Bernard Fredericks was born in Liverpool. He is a freelance writer; also, he has contributed to a multiplicity of published articles to various magazines, newspapers, and on occasions, local radio. He was also an active member of a Northwest Writers' Club, and for some years served as an editor of a monthly arts magazine published in North West England.

He released his first book of WWII trilogy about Liverpool kids during WWII, entitled *The Green Gates Story-Escape from the Blitz*.

Second publication is *Liverpool Kids of WWII,* Part 1 – *After the Blitz*. This latest and final publication of the trilogy is *Liverpool Kids of WWII, Part 2 – Beyond the Blitz*.

He is married with a grown-up family and presently residing in North Wales, where he's working on new scripts for future publication.

To a city which has spawned and bred its hard-working masses who believe in themselves, and display a gritty preparedness in maturity. When threatened, will unflinchingly stare adversity in the face and in defiance, take on all comers!

And its young people, like their parents, possessing a ready wit and who are easily moved to humour, and are generous with regard to strangers.

Most importantly, they also have a built-in flexibility in that when they err or make mistakes – as all are wont to do at times – are capable of standing back to laugh at their own absurdities and themselves, if need be.

Bernard Fredericks

# LIVERPOOL KIDS OF WWII, PART 2

Beyond the Blitz

**AUSTIN MACAULEY PUBLISHERS**™
LONDON • CAMBRIDGE • NEW YORK • SHARJAH

Copyright © Bernard Fredericks 2022

The right of Bernard Fredericks to be identified as author of this work has been asserted by the author in accordance with sections 77 and 78 of the Copyright, Designs and Patents Act 1988.

All rights reserved. No part of this publication may be reproduced, stored in a retrieval system, or transmitted in any form or by any means, electronic, mechanical, photocopying, recording, or otherwise, without the prior permission of the publishers.

Any person who commits any unauthorised act in relation to this publication may be liable to criminal prosecution and civil claims for damages.

This is a work of fiction. Names, characters, businesses, places, events, locales, and incidents are either the products of the author's imagination or used in a fictitious manner. Any resemblance to actual persons, living or dead, or actual events is purely coincidental.

A CIP catalogue record for this title is available from the British Library.

ISBN 9781398423084 (Paperback)
ISBN 9781398423091 (ePub e-book)

www.austinmacauley.com

First Published 2022
Austin Macauley Publishers Ltd®
1 Canada Square
Canary Wharf
London
E14 5AA

Once again, would like to thank the technical staff of the AM Production Team and other associates at Austin Macauley Publishers for assisting and advising me during the production phases of this publication and for her support and patience during the long arduous months of the recent world-wide contagion.

Other works by Bernard Fredericks

1. *WRITERS WORLD*
*(History of Liverpool Writers' club 1922 – 1994)*
ISBN 9781906823672 - 2013

2. *THE GREEN GATES STORY*
*(Escape from the Liverpool Blitz)*
ISBN 9781786126856 - 2017

3. *FLEETING IMAGES from a Bloodied Past*
*(A Dimension of Laird's Navy)*
ISBN 9781788782357 - 2020

4. *LIVERPOOL KIDS OF WWII Part 1*
*(After The Blitz)*
ISBN 9781528918466 - 2020

5. *Liverpool Kids Of WWII Part 2*
*(Beyond The Blitz)*
*ISBN 9781398423084 - 2022*

## War News!

- British Forces defeat Japanese troops under Lt. Gen. Mutaguchi, attempting to overrun and swamp the defences at Kohima, Burma, and continue their drive into India. Heavy enemy casualties were estimated to be in the region of 70,000 dead.

# 1. New Brighton Open Air Baths

"So, what are we gonna do today?" one tired voice almost yawned. The September Road gang were sat chatting to each other during a boring mid-morning get-together.

The North Wales holiday was a week old and now history. Conversation and recall of incidents, humorous and otherwise, had waned and become exhausted, forgotten.

The great thing they all shared was that the school holidays were still to be enjoyed, so that there was still time to do whatever they liked?

He stared out of the front room window, and up between the drawn-back curtains, at an empty scene and a clear cloudless blue sky that was full of promise.

Like it was gonna be a warm day, and no rain to put a dampener on things.

It was a good feeling he had.

He breathed contentedly and even smiled at his own reflection in the window-glass that bounced back at him.

No more, shouted commands from the foot of the stairs penetrating sweet dreams in the cold grey of an early winter dawn, like, "YOU UP YET!" More a command than a question.

No more having to face the stomach-churning ordeal and steam-laden air of school dinners in the main hall!

No more – an' best of all – home work!

Mmm…but there was a blip, or if you like/prefer, a cloud on the horizon: no let-up in the weekly piano lessons, a considered infringement on his precious leisure time.

He shook his head. He'd left the house and wandered up the road to join a group of his pals he'd spotted, loitering and lounging around on the pavement in front of one of their houses.

"Me mam…" interrupted one of the four boys in a sing-song voice. On this occasion, there were two girls of twelve years sat amongst the boys in a line on the long low stone brick wall which fronted the properties, each concerned with their own bored thoughts. Behind them a narrow strip of sparse over-grown and weed-infested garden, mostly fronted with ragged, overgrown and untended untidy privets.

"Your mam? What about her?" one of them said, picking him up on his utterance.

She said, "Why don't us kids all go to the New Brighton open-air baths?" he continued.

This was followed by silence, while this snippet of advice was digested, and during which, one or the other reached up an idle hand to rub a furrowed forehead, ruefully, scratch away in the thatch of unruly hair on their heads or force a finger down an itchy ear-hole and wiggle the nail to catch any brown wax, which hadn't been removed when supposedly washing themselves that morning.

"I s'pose," one voice began.

One of the girls slid off her perch and stood in front and facing them, hands on hips from her feet-apart stance on the pavement above a hop-scotch pattern in white faded chalk still barely visible on the dry flags beneath her brown leather sandals.

"Why don't we ALL go?" she urged, her voice full of expectant excitement.

"How much?" a misery with drooping shoulders mumbled, sat amongst the boys on one end.

"We went there, couple o' weeks ago," ventured a voice, "an' I think it was only about a tanner(3P) to get in, during the week."

"Then there's the tram fare to get down to the Pier Head?" the same tired voice queried.

"Scholar's Return," suggested another, shifting off the wall and adding his personal view on the matter.

"What about the ferry over to New Brighton?"

"Shillin'(5p), there-n'-back, I shouldn't wonder," commented an enlightened voice.

So it was agreed then, they all unanimously nodded, warming to the subject.

They scattered off the wall and away home to collect towels, cosies and spare cash, before returning to their meeting area, where the adventure had been discussed.

He left his mum a note on the kitchen table, telling her where he was going, just in case she returned home early from work and wondered why he wasn't home.

They walked quickly off in a purposeful noisy group and caught a No. 29 tram going into town, charging noisily upstairs to grab the seats nearest to the front, all full of excitement and the fact that they were going somewhere, and best of all, because they'd decided collectively to do it just like older kids in their teens might.

Conductor wasn't best pleased; them charging past him up the stairs, because he had to climb those stairs himself to collect their fares.

They enjoyed the feeling of exerting their new-found confidence in reaching a decision collectively and to exercise their capabilities.

It was a fine day, but a brisk breezily westerly wind greeted them down at the Pier Head as they stepped down to the landing stage and then crossed the lowered gangway onto the moored Mersey Ferry, which would transport them up river to New Brighton.

When, on board the ferry, he took his leave of the other kids as they raced up the steps to the top deck. First of all, he headed around the waist of the vessel, until he found the exposed, but railed off, companionway, leading down to the engine room spaces. He leaned on the cross rope to peer down into the brightly lit, but smelly and noisy engine room.

It excited him, like when he'd stood alongside the locomotive on one of the platforms at Liverpool's Lime Street Station. The giant-sized engine was – at that time – manned by two burly engineers, staring down at him from the cabin behind the controls and furnace opening under the boiler.

It was all there – these scenes – encapsulated, riveting and exciting.

They didn't walk from New Brighton Landing Stage, after alighting from the ferry, because they wouldn't and couldn't delay their headlong rush – racing each other – to the pay box at the entrance to the open-air baths. The sun was shining with barely a cloud in the bright blue sky, plus even the fresh air smelt good: a brisk salted odour blowing gently off the Irish Sea.

They caused frowns from employees at the Baths as they collided with each other racing headlong to the boy/girl changing rooms, after rushing through the pay box turnstiles. They tore their clothing off, rather than undress, at top speed, stepped and dragged on their swim-wear. Loose garments were snatched up off the floor and thrust under-arm as they vacated the cubicles to search for a locker; then legging it headlong for the water's edge of the gigantic three-hundred-thirty-foot-wide pool, with the shallow end starting at zero depth to three feet where most of the kids were frolicking.

He'd never visited New Bright Baths before joining his pals, this day, to go visit, so he had looked forward to it. He'd heard that it was only opened five years before the war? Although, it must be said, every kid on both sides of the river knew about it, because they'd heard grown-ups praising its proportions. He sighed with satisfaction because they weren't wrong. No, sirree! A wonderful and great place for water thrills and lotsa fun!

Yes, and even the water gave off a clean and pure odour.

Beat swimming at Lister Drive Liverpool Corporation swimming baths, yes sir!

The girls joined them, testing the water tentatively with their toes – shrieking with thrilled delight – and were then immediately targeted in a charge by the boys, scooping up sprays of – at first – chilling cold heavy drops. At close range, they now kicked volumes of ankle-deep sheets of exploding droplets, which thoroughly drenched the girl's previously dry costumes and sent them into a screaming huddle of failed protection.

After the initial excitement, they went around the pool, which was pilling up rapidly with other young bathers, including baby-paddlers shielded from their shenanigans by protective mums-n'-dads, as they were urged and coxed into taking their first gleeful steps in the shallows, held upright from their over-the-head extended arms, hands and wrists firmly held by their pops or mums, right behind them. The dads barefoot with the trouser-bottoms folded up and some sporting white handkerchiefs adjusted to protect bald and exposed pates.

The group soon discovered the low water slides, and spent time and energy dashing to the foot of the steps leading up to the junior platforms at the head of the slides, jumping into a seated position and then shoving hard with both hands, catapulting down and into the three-foot shallows, sinking beneath with a tremendous thrilling splash, which found them sitting on the bottom with a ruffled surface twelve inches about them, to which they rose in an instant as they launched 'themselves upwards, both feet planted firmly on the bottom of the pool and legs propelling them toward the sun-kissed rippling surface and fresh air.

One of the boys had his seven-year-old little brother in tow. His mum, so he moaned gave him an ultimatum: *'He goes with you. I'm not having him left in the house on his own. Your dad and me's at work. – If you don't take him, you stay here!'*

At New Brighton open air baths, the children's small slide was built on the edge at the three-foot depth. They could see it was in constant use. The younger brother was urged to 'move himself' and get up the metal ladder, then climb up onto the slide, but he refused. Said he was frightened. The boy's older brother turned to his peers with raised shoulders and eyebrows, inviting help.

"Okay, I'll take him up and slide down with him," the boy's closest pal agreed.

The youngster was calmed as he took the willing hand, helping him mount the ladder of the low-level frame. Soon as he got onto the platform, he sat down beside him with a comforting arm around the little fellah's shoulders, ready for the slide down and into the three-foot end of the pool.

But this didn't suit the boy and instead – on his own initiative – clambered up onto his brother's best mate, both arms encircling the older boy's neck and clinging to his back like a school satchel.

"Okay, if your want," the bigger boy allowed over his shoulder.

He launched himself forward and down the short metal slide into the water, crashing through the surface with a big splash and was almost immediately landing bottom first on the submerged pool floor. He flexed his legs and thighs to raise himself up off it, but instantly realised that wasn't possible as the youngster on his back, gripped him more tightly around the neck for safety as his little head sank down below the surface.

The older lad hadn't accounted for the extra weight. This weight – little though it was – was sufficient to prevent him from positioning his underwater balance as he prepared to stand. In this moment of shock, he reached up, grabbed the youngster's wrists and wrestled to part them. The grip around his throat intensified as the frightened youngster held on for dear life! And that was exactly what the older boy knew he must quickly do something about. Their below water tangle was only seconds, but he recognised instantly how dangerous and perilous his position – THEIR POSITION – was. He twisted sideways, thrust a hand and arm hard down against the floor of the pool and forced himself frantically upright. Coughing and spluttering, the water cascading from their bodies, they broke surface together.

His friends were howling in fits of hysterical laughter, clearly not aware of how close this little incident had come to turning into an afternoon of tragedy.

They couldn't get enough of it, and repeatedly strode briskly, sometimes falling over in their haste from the shallows to gain the side of the pool, hauling their dripping skinny, shiny torsos up onto terra-firma and racing yet again for the slide to clamber up and onto the raised wet-deck platform.

Only when they were happily exhausted did they pause and stop to catch their breath, sitting in a line on the edge of the three-foot end, feet dangling in the lovely fresh salt bath waters, but only to catch their breath.

They sat in a laughing chatting huddle together, on the tiled steps at the edge of the pool watching, listening and sometimes pointing at the antics of others around them on a sunny afternoon.

He, as per usual, felt the cold. Some would smirk and call him 'nesh' or sensitive to cold. Certainly, he would quickly produce goose-pimples on his skin. He was okay in the water, running around the pool playing tick, but when he sat down and the breeze blew – however lightly – he immediately felt it and reached for his towel. Was not fond, let it be said, of the cold, whether it be snow-n'-ice in the winter months or a cool penetrating easterly in the summer. One or two of the other kids showed similar signs and threw their towels over their bare shoulder and back. Not yet at the shivering stage, but he could 'murder' a bacon butty!

Then a little miracle occurred. One of the girls produced a cloth-wrapped item, inside of which, when she opened it out on her knees, was a small already cut stack of tasty marmalade sandwiches. She offered them around, just a one-half square to each, although sticky, but who cared? It would wash off their fingers in the pool.

It was a joyful delight, a Godsend to their starving digestion. Unfortunately, all too quickly devoured.

"You try the springy, yet?" one of the boys asked the others. There were giggles and shakes of the head.

One of the girls turned to him as he tried to wrap his towel ever closer around his rib cage.

"What about you?" she teased.

"Me?" he gagged, amazed to be asked.

"Yes, you," she continued, both girls smiling behind the challenge.

"This is the first time I've ever been here!" he defended.

"That doesn't matter, and besides, there's alwus a first time?"

"I've seen yuh go off the board in Lister Drive Baths," accused one of the boys, a school classmate.

He pursed his lips before replying. "That was the only springy in there."

"What difference does that make?"

"Like I said," he retorted.

"Oh," the girl next to him screeched, "so you've been off one already?"

"Not here," he defended.

This was greeted and drowned out with a chorus of huzzas and half-boos.

"G'wan, let's see you dive off the low board?" one of the girls dared him.

He chanced a speculate glance toward where the towering diving boards were clustered: low board, next to medium, and the top board overlooking the fifteen-foot end of the pool.

"C'mon, yoos can do it?" the boys mischievously urged.

"Only off the low board, and jus' this once!" he insisted, reluctantly cornered, climbing to his feet and dropping his towel in the middle of them.

There was a short volley of cheers and clapping as he left them to walk around the edge of the pool toward the terrace and café, to where the diving boards were clustered.

When he arrived at the foot of the diving board's structure, he glanced back toward his friends, and they gave him a wave to let him know he was being watched, scrutinised and under their surveillance, in case he tried to change his mind.

A stupid and dangerous thought entered his mind. There were just a few people about by the boards, and it occurred to him, seeing as how they were goading him, to call their bluff instead, and show off. Besides, he was curious about what the world looked like, up there, but for no other reason.

He arched his head to glance up above his head and then stepped over to the metal ladders and began to climb. Up he went to the middle board, his destination, then – because it didn't look much higher – carried on climbing to the top board, just to see how high it really was, with no intention in mind. It could be a good topic to talk about when he got back down and joined his mates – the height and what he could see from there, that is.

Thing was, when he got up and stood at the back of the 25/30-foot-high board, and glanced down, he was shocked at how high it really was! He licked his suddenly dry lips and decided at least he'd wave in their direction, before turning around to descend the ladder.

"Hurry up, kid!" he thought he heard someone shout.

He looked down through the safety rails and saw below him dressed in white shirt and pants, a Bath Attendant staring up at him, hands on his hips, his face flushed and waiting. So, too, he noticed were about twenty to thirty others, upturned faces, watching him also, some in mild curiosity together with a group of burly lads in their mid to late teens, being waved back by the attendant. Yet another attendant was waving swimmers in the water below the boards to move away and to give the 'young fellah' on the top board space and room to make his dive.

He gasped in surprise and not a little consternated at the audience gathered below.

"Hurry up, we can't wait all day!" the stern-faced attendant shouted, yet again.

This wasn't what he had in mind when he began the climb. Glancing at the board and gauging the distance of the drop, made his blood run cold.

It was higher than he'd thought.

Like standing on the edge of a coastal cliff!

"AY! YOU UP THERE!" the voice raised, turning impatient.

Instantly, he realised he couldn't climb back down the ladder.

The whole world was bloody-well watching!

He was faced with a suicidal decision!

He cringed, his mouth dry, and stepped away from the rail on wobbly legs and started along the thin board toward the end, conscious that it seemed to have shrunk to being only six inches wide!

His legs trembled and felt like jelly. There was every likelihood and danger that he'd start to wobble some more and fall off sideways, before he got any further, and finish up on the concrete.

This was madness!

There was not time to think as he tottered to the end of the board and forced himself to jump…

The surface of the water rushed up toward him. Was so hard as his backside crashed onto it in one awesome massive splash, then sinking down in a rush into the darkness and gloom of the pool at the bottom of the fifteen-foot depth together with a rush of trapped air bubbles. Even in shock, his mind registered wonder at the amount of green moss or seaweed, whatever, his feet touched down upon as he came to a stop. Blind fright and panic made his leg muscles launch himself up off the slimy bottom toward the distant lighted surface. His lungs devoid of air after it was all knocked out of him when he crashed onto the surface screamed for replenishment. His shocked mind was focussed on the thought that drowning was never more present than the here-and-now!

He struck out and clawed his way up and broke the surface, swallowing a mouthful of bath water, gasping for air and in no position to hear and appreciate the applause from the small gathering who witnessed his 'event' at poolside.

Back with his mates and somewhat recovered from his ordeal, he accepted their congratulations with a fake shrug but carefully concealed his real inner candid thoughts of how close he'd come to his demise and promising himself there would NEVER be a repetition of this mentally disordered insanity ever again.

However, his 'bravery' was chattered about and reported to the rest of the kids in the road, when they returned home, and was spoken about for almost a week afterwards.

He bathed blissfully in the hollow distinction.

### War News!

- Polish underground resistance fighters (Home Army) stage an orchestrated and organised uprising in the Polish capital, Warsaw, as Soviet army spearheads pierce rear-guard German army units defending their retreat from the country. Assault has started on key strategic installations throughout the city…

## 2. Pears as Big as Hand-Bells

Back to sitting hunched and perched on the low wall front of the houses on September Road, like a bunch of starlings, 'chewing the cud' and chatting enjoyable rubbish again, between themselves, which always initiated laughs and witty comments.

The escapade at New Brighton open air swimming baths was history, and no longer a subject worth discussing.

"You must be able to see them pear trees from the back of your's?" one of the lads said to him as he kicked the loose tennis ball back and forth across the empty pavement to hit the wall and bounce back to him.

"What pears?" he replied, not particularly interested in the topic.

"Them pear trees at the back of your's?"

"Pear trees?" he questioned, trapping the bounce of the ball under the sole of his left shoe.

"Jeeze!" said his questioner, turning to the others on the wall. "Here's a kid who doesn't know what's over the wall from his own back garden," glancing sideways with pained incredulity, and then accusing. "Don't you ever look over your back wall, at all?"

"For what?"

"Just told yuh: pears?"

"You mean, in the back garden of the houses on Breckside Park Road?"

"WELL! Well!" said the other, his head sideways to catch the eyes of the other kids. "Penny's dropped, at last."

Becoming focussed, he responded. "Okay, so they've got a few pear trees in their back garden, so what?"

"You seen how big they are?"

"Not that interested."

The other chuckled, with yet again a glance and a wink, this time, at the other boys. "You might not, but WE are."

"So?"

"So, how long have them ripe pears been hanging there?"

"Told you, I'm not that interested."

"Well, we is," the other boys chorused in unison, with raised eyebrows, and then to each other, "ain't we?"

They grinned and chorused louder, this time in unison and confirmation.

"So, what are you suggesting?"

"Them pears have been hanging on them trees for weeks, an' they're biggies, hand-bell size."

"How d'you know this?"

"'Cause I seen 'em!"

"When?"

"When I come to yours, an' we played kick-about on the grass in your back garden. Your mum called you in and while you were gone, I got up on the wall to take a good look."

"The people over there," he insisted, haughtily, "are probably waiting until they get big and ripe, then they'll pluck or pick them off the trees, whatever?"

"Yeah, but," questioner said, his eyes gleaming as he sought to involve them in his conspiracy scheme. "What if – we picked them first?"

"That's stealing," he dismissed.

"Listen to Holy Joe, here?"

"Well, it is!" he insisted, slightly uneasy about the implication and the way the discussion was going.

"If they don't want them, an' leave 'em on the tree until they falls off, and then rot away on the ground, that's a crime."

"Their trees. They can do what they like."

"He's their mouth-piece, as well!" the other accused, pointing an accusing finger on an extended arm, back at him.

"He's right," another voice chimed in. "We could eat them pears, then they wouldn't be goin' to waste, like he said."

"Hey," added his accuser. "The government said, 'Waste Not, Want Not!'"

He shook his head. "It's a proverb."

There was a moment of distinct silence.

"What's a proverb?" one asked, innocently, in a sing-song voice.

"Like a timed piece of advice – something we advise all the time and often."

The boy at centre stage waved a dismissive hand and further argued. "No matter. Listen, the government are telling' us we shouldn't waste food, right?"

Instead of replying, he released the ball from under his left shoe and kicked it at the wall, waiting for it to bounce back.

"He knows what you're talkin' about," another voice called out, agreeing with 'rescuing' the pears.

"So what about it?" the chief conspirator challenged.

He kicked the ball as it bounced back off the wall and returned to him, stood at the kerb, waiting and watching its motion. He trapped it under his shoe, again.

"Okay, but don't take the lot! An'," he warned, "I don't want you comin' 'round to my house, when me mum's in!"

That got a wide grin of success. "What are we waitin' for, boys?" the lad continued, clapping both hands together in glee and anticipation.

Mum and Dad were at work. He knew that and so did his mates in the road, especially this lot on the wall, so he couldn't use that as an excuse for refusing them entry to his back garden.

He led the way up his side path from the pavement to his side gate, the other three trooping along in Indian file, behind him; then across what 'passed' for a rear lawn. Silently, they arrived at the back red sandstone wall overlooking a back garden to one of the houses with fronts facing Breck Park Road.

The only obstacle, if it could be called as such, was a black-n'-white Tom-cat, sitting on the wall, it's paws folded back and under its chest, observing their approach through hooded eyes and not a little suspiciously, the tail beginning to snake back-n'-forth.

They silently looked over and beyond the top of the wall. Nothing stirred. No movement, not even at the back windows to the house, and that included the kitchen windows, which – of course – overlooked the garden and the pear trees, within that enclosure.

It was mid-afternoon and midweek, so no activity was seen nor expected. They reached forward, their bony sinewy hands securing firm grip on the smooth top of the wall and launched themselves up and astride of it.

Their feline observer, fled.

He had grave doubts about trespassing into the next garden, especially from his own. He didn't have to think about what Mum would say, if she was aware of this intent, but he couldn't see any way out of it. He'd been trapped by their cunning and so was forced to go along with it.

Duress?

The boys dropped lightly and furtively into the private garden with the fruit trees no more than ten feet away. They made straight for the pear trees, and he noticed that there was an abundance of mature fruit, both lying abandoned in the overgrown grass beneath them, as well as on the branches overhanging.

"These on the ground, look okay," he murmured drawing their attention and quietly hoping they'd collect them first, which looked like the lesser evil to picking them straight off the tree.

The pears were certainly very mature, being as big as hand bells as he'd been led to believe, from amid the foot-high tufts of wild growing grass, at the foot of the trees – some seven or so, in all.

They'd just about picked up as many as they could possibly handle, when the back door to the property was suddenly wrenched open and a grey-haired, stooped old man, walking stick in hand, appeared in the open doorway.

"Hey!" he shouted.

One, the boys straightened up to behold the figure stood at the door opening. Almost on cue, they turned and fled for the wall and safety.

"HEY!" the old man yelled, yet again, this time waving his stick in the air, but by now they were flying like hares and halfway to the wall, one or two of the collected pears already slipping, falling from their grasp and bouncing in the long grass.

"YOU THERE!" they heard his croaky voice, as he stepped onto the gravel path at his back door.

However, they'd reached the wall and clambered up and over it, clutching the remains of their ill-gotten gains. They fell in an excited giggling heap in his back garden, from where they started from, and because they were making so much noise themselves, didn't hear the old man's shouted message.

"You can have them dropped pears…Didn't have to sneak in an' steal 'em…I'd 'ave given 'em away, anyhow…"

They didn't look back over the wall, because they didn't want him to get a good look at their faces, didn't see the old man shake his head, breathe a heavy sigh and stumble back in doors.

He knew and boys were sure, – they wouldn't be back.

### War News!

- Two-thousand-year-old city of Rennes, capital of Brittany, is liberated by General Patton's Third US Army and in particular units of Brig General Benjamin Davis, entered the city.

- French resistance stage an uprising in Paris as Allied armies advance on the city.
- Allied troops invade southern France as part of Operation Dragoon.
- US Marine Corps and Army retake Guam from the Japanese, in the Mariana Islands.

# 3. Shiny Chain on a Pretty Ankle

The boys of his gang, during their rare chat and discussions about the opposite gender – girls, or 'gerls' as they were won't to refer to in pure Scouse dialect, raised the 'deadly sin' subject they'd overheard their older siblings speak of. Especially when their tongues were loosened after a few pints. Namely women-of-the-night, fancy ladies, those of 'easy virtue' who only kissed for dosh!

"Sinners?" smirked one.

One of the girls – sister to one of the gang – said. "My mum said they're husband stealers!"

"Not alwus," protested one of the boys, after the girls had departed. "Cos, I heard me bruther telling' one of his mates that they go with anyone!"

"What does that mean?" another voice chirped up.

"Don't have to be married, like."

"But," interrupted another, "the fellahs who are married could pretend they wasn't?"

"Yeah!" was a chorus of excited voices, followed by a silence that was broken by a burst of bewildered laughter.

"Them pictures in Lilliput. – Are dey deese ladies-of-the night?"

"Where d'you get dis ladies-of-the-night, malarkey from?"

"Well, I heard me bruder sayin' they on'y comes out at night," the boy replied.

In a flash, another said. "Like owls, yeah?"

"Where?" questioned an eager voice.

"Where what?" a naïve whisper ventured.

"Where does ladies-of-the-night come out, arsehole?"

"In town, someplace," shrugged the face supplying the intelligence, and added. "Just outside the boosers by the back-entry jiggers."

"Is that where the fellahs go for a kiss-an'-a-cuddle?"

"Sounds, the gear!" cackled a high-pitched voice. "Got me all of a doodar…"

"Get him!" screeched the boy alongside derisively, followed by a chorus of erupted laughter, but had them all glancing quickly over their shoulders and around, to make sure they weren't overheard by passing grown-ups.

The short discussion trailed off for want of further informed comment, but it was accepted that they – the women of the night – would be recognised by the little gold chain they wore on one ankle. Thought, suddenly struck him, which one? But then, he dismissed the question, because it didn't seem to matter. Chain, didn't really have to be gold, for instance, could've been silver – or even brass, they agreed.

As he sat next to his mum, going into town clanking along on an old bone-shaker tram, which had seats that were really benches facing each other along both side of the downstairs saloon. His bored eyes were to become startled as they caught sight of and came into contact at the across-the-aisle woman's ankle. Dangling down from the shapely ankle was a tiny thin shiny metal chain, fastened loosely around one of her ankles above a high-heel glossy-black leather shoe. His curiosity forced his head to rise, and his vision travelled up her bare legs to the hem of her short skirt, then to see both hands clasped together securely on her handbag, holding it firmly against her flat stomach. His eyes continued to move upwards over her ample bosom, a slim, smooth firm throat, dimpled chin and – a beautifully smiling face which hovered and rose into view, like the radiance of an early morning sunrise.

He instantly noted the lipstick, eye-shadow and other cosmetic applications, just like an attractive film star – Rita Heyworth look-a-like?

Shock-horror! Oh God, she was watching him, he observed with a jolt!

He made conscious effort to stare down at the bare-boards of the floor beneath his feet.

He was completely overwhelmed by her startling good looks and she had those big beautiful 'lamps' of blue eyes, – and focused upon him: just feet away across the aisle.

He chanced his hand with another glimpse at her.

There was glancing eye-contact.

She winked at him…!

His mouth dried up with shock, and he darted a sidelong startled glance at his mum to see if she had picked it up, taking this all in, and wondering why this stunning apparition opposite should be interested in her twelve-year-old little boy?

It was about this time that his nostrils activated and sent electric messages to his brain: her scent – or as it was called in the films, perfume, had wafted over him as the conductor stepped between them drawing a sweep of air by the passage of movement, and hurried to the front of the car to collect fares.

Was his mum aware of all this?

She wasn't or didn't seem or show to be. He was relieved to confirm this and concentrated on staring down again at the floor of the dirty old tram-car avoiding with great difficulty the urge to glance back up again and chance his hand – yet again – without another swift glance in her direction across the aisle.

Was she…? He hesitated, guessing the word and wetting his lips and becoming very uncomfortable and puzzlingly anxious.

When the tram halted at a city tram stop, he was aware that she had slid off her seat and alighted down the exit steps from the tramcar and onto the cobbled roadway.

His head turned and his eyes tracked her movement.

An elbow nudged his startled side shoulder nearest to his mum.

"Did you know that girl?" his mother whispered to him in a hushed voice, not quite a whisper.

"No, er, no," he vigorously denied, embarrassed to be caught out eyeing her.

"So, why were you staring at her?" his mother persisted.

"Staring?" he refuted, a little too loudly, the decibels rising.

"Sh! Shush! No need to tell the world!" she cautioned with a smile.

"I…No…" he mumbled in confusion.

"That's all right then. Just that I caught you staring at her out of the corner of my eye?"

He shook his head rapidly to convince her.

He now knew, he had been caught out!

Staring anywhere around on the lower deck of the rattling tramcar, was more important, rather than making eye-contact with his mum. He always had the uncanny feeling that when they did – and there was a fib involved – she could mysteriously see and read right through and into what he was thinking.

He couldn't have asked: 'Mum, what does it mean when a lady wears an ankle chain?'

And, while the girl/woman was sat especially within hearing distance?

Definitely a no-no, for more than one reason.

Upon reflection, he wished he was suddenly older, but dismissed the thought as a load of cods-wallop!

As his mum was now confronted by the conductor for the fares, she searched for her purse in her handbag, which allowed him the chance to throw a final glance out through the back window of the tram as it began to move off, and he stole a sideways glimpse back at her receding figure: a curl of blond hair blowing in a slight breeze which lifted gently off her forehead, her shoulder-length hair swishing briefly, – at a rapidly extending distance – as the tram wheels squealed in resumed forward momentum toward at the next bend in the road.

The scene changed, and this vision of her was lost from view.

He frowned as he recalled his mate's comments and the reference to the ankle chain and their smirking interpretation.

Were they right?

An' how did their brothers come to make that kinda definition? – Did they know somebody like that – one of these girls?

This one, who'd been sat opposite, on the tram, was too good for that shower, he sourly concluded.

He was uncomfortable with the questions that had sprung to mind.

She didn't look furtive, double-dealing or deceitful.

Didn't accept their eavesdropped definition.

Why not, he asked himself?

Truth was, he didn't want to believe or accept his view of people could be so wrong.

Mum had asked – 'Did he know her?'

He wished he did, he told himself, enjoying the temporary amusement of a silent and private remembrance and which now turned more serious…

Was suddenly aware of a powerful emotion and extraordinary feeling, and she – this woman, young woman- had triggered it.

A strangeness had come – overtaken him – and he was uneasy in its clutches because it was new-ish and puzzlingly came out of nowhere! Reminded him of how he felt about his young lady teacher, back in Warton, when he'd been evacuated. That strange feeling which had took hold and attracted him to her…

Its rippling perplexity unnerved and disturbed his thinking, which wasn't normal – this feeling, that is.

Because he didn't or wouldn't identify it and couldn't put a name to it, teased and agitated his normal, well…He considered himself, one-of-the-boys with uniform street-cred composure.

Was conscious of hazy feelings: losing out, missing something and falling behind – self-pity and all, tangled up together? A mishmash? Was aware that he was on the edge of something confusing because it was indefinable.

He was glad Mum didn't guess what was in his thoughts, and which he now sought to rid from mind, together with the connected anxiety that threatened to engulf him. He concentrated, instead, on what game or games, he and his mates would get up to that night? This worked, because this present mixed-up thinking seemed to resume normality and in so doing to flush out the flash disturbance of the last few minutes!

But, at the end of those minutes he'd remembered her presence.

In his young mind, she was startlingly beautiful.

Stunning! Yep, a new word he'd picked up while sitting in the local flea-pit watching some soppy film, where young men in the film were referring to a local actress on screen.

He liked picking up new words and phrases and using them, 'specially when he noticed that the use of them would draw the attention of adults, who usually regarded most kids – not all, mark you – as inarticulate and ignorant…which, upon further personal reflection, he resentfully had to agree, because he knew he was one of them!

His mind shifted back to the present and the thought emerged: If he was suddenly old enough?

Sighed dramatically to himself, but not loud enough for his mum's shell-likes.

Not for him, sadly.

Out of his reach…unhappily.

Still in short pants!

And, only just twelve years old…

His thinking was changing, too. Girls, he supposed, were not completely, – well, nuisances.

He knew, there was more to them than that, but was unsure of what that might be?

**War News!**

- Russian army takes the city of Bucharest, advancing from the east.
- Uprising continues in Warsaw against German occupation, as Russian forces arrive on the outskirts.

# 4. Surprise Weekend Away!

It was fun to ride up on his bike to visit Vee's house, not only because Majorie lived next door, or that sometimes Mrs Sherry, Vee's mum, would want to see a film at the local flea-pit: West Derby Picture House and take him with her. Wasn't really a flea-pit and he liked the seating arrangement, because it all sloped down from the back at a nice angle, and just about everybody could easily see the screen. Her husband, Mr Sherry, was in the Railway Police. He wasn't always home to take her and go with her, as much as he would have liked to have done.

Vee was still writing and receiving soppy grown-up letters, he imaged, from his big brother in the army, so when he rode up to visit with any flimsy excuse used, he could always reckon on a friendly and genuine welcome.

As well as countless cups of hot milk and a biscuit or two to dunk in it, there was always the chance that Mrs Sherry would invite him to escort her down to the West Derby Picture House in the village. She, of course, always paid for both of them. First House or early evening show, so he could get off home afterwards, without it being too late in the evening.

The awful incident, not that long ago, in which he had been responsible for the early death of her pet dog due to a RTA, had been quietly set aside and he was forgiven for his inexperience in dog-walking, which had led to the poor little mutt's demise.

Vee's dad, who he was relaxingly urged to call 'Uncle Jim' was a large, barrel-chested man in his fifties, always seemed cheerful with a red beefy face, but never hardly seemed to be at home, when he called. Maybe, it was because he worked night's down at the Central Rail Station in town, and therefore, would be asleep upstairs on the occasions that he called by. Vee had a job working in a nearby Rail Station Ticket Office. Like most girls of working age, she was faced with the option of being a Land Army Girl, working in munitions factories or being a member of the Women Services, or being employed in a strategic capacity, all because all eligible men of military age were already called up to serve The Colours.

Like most, and no different than any other British girl of her age, she'd get a bit fed-up with having to meet her work place responsibilities and needed – from time to time – a bit of a change. So, when a long weekend came up, and a relative in North Wales had invited the family, previously to come over and stay whenever they wanted, she decided to take them up on the offer. Problem was, her boyfriend – big brother – was in the army and away, and her close local girlfriend was working, that weekend.

"D'you think your mum would lend you to me over next weekend?" Vee teased him.

"Lend me?" he frowned, sat next to and between Vee and Mrs Sherry on the sofa with a large hot cup of cocoa gripped tightly between both his hands.

"To come with me as a – well, chaperon, to Colwyn Bay?"

He'd heard of the place, but never been there and knew that it was a long way away by Crossville bus or by train, but he was immediately eager, – no, delighted!

So it was decided that Vee and her mother would speak to his mum about his travelling to the North Wales resort by train that coming weekend, leaving and staying over Friday and Saturday nights, returning late Sunday afternoon.

Mum even supplied a little suitcase containing clean, freshly ironed clothes and pocket money to spend, whilst there.

All exciting stuff!

Vee and him, had rushed down into town that Friday noon-time to catch a train at Central Station underground. Uncle Jim, Vee's dad, met them in his police uniform and then saw them off safely from the right platform onto a train that would commute to Chester Station, where they'd change to catch another headed for Llandudno Junction, but – of course – dismounting at Colwyn Bay.

With a slip of paper torn from the top of yesterday's Liverpool Echo newspaper, bearing the handwritten address in Vee's hand, they left the platform and out of the station, she gripping his hand and tugging him along in tow with his suitcase banging and colliding with the back of his legs.

"D'you know where you're going?" he asked her, a tad anxious about her indecisiveness of direction once they were arrived in the centre of this hilly seaside town.

She stopped an elderly couple for directions, and when they looked bewildered and unsure, showed them the written address. P'raps, it was the way Vee pronounced the Welsh worded address that had the couple conferring, but whatever, as soon as she showed it to them, that part of the riddle was soon cleared up. The couple quickly pointed out the direction they should take and the route to follow.

It was uphill, as it were, all the way in the residential area that backed-up from the water's-edge, and the railway station. Finally, puffing and blowing a bit, Vee paused in front of a terraced house with low wall behind which was a brief tiny stretch of garden. She skipped up the couple of polished tile steps and knocked, not at all sure this was the house they'd be staying at? All was happily relieved when the door opened and there was immediate recognition on the doorstep.

They were both welcomed in and informed that their 'Tea' had already been laid in anticipation. All they needed to do was step into the hall, depositing their hand luggage at the foot of the stairs, which led to the upper bedrooms of the dwelling. They were Immediately escorted through the hallway and into the sitting room, and gestured to sit down and commence to eat, which sounded like a boss idea to him, because after what he considered to have been a long train journey, he was 'starving'!

After the meal and while the conversation buzzed back-n-forth across the table, he walked over to the window, but was in for a shock. When he glanced out, expecting the yard and a back gate, he instead was amazed to find he was forced to stare out and down through the window into a narrow, paved yard some many feet below the outside ledge.

He knew they'd entered the house, straight from the road outside, through the front door into the hall, where they'd deposited their baggage, were led into the sitting room where they ate, and all on the same floor level.

He remembered passing a stairway leading upstairs. Now, without climbing those stairs, he was looking down into the back yard – a drop of twenty to twenty-five feet. He couldn't understand why?

How come?

He stepped back from the window and even said as much, out loud. This halted the conversation at the table behind him.

There was a pause as the words sunk in, followed instantly by an excited laugh from Vee's relatives.

"That's because the house was built on the side of a hill," explained one.

He had to go see for himself. Retraced his steps into the hall, down to the front door, opened it briefly and looked out at the level of short outside front path to the closed gate, pavement and tarmacadamed roadway beyond, as though to confirm his understanding. He closed, shut the door and returned down the hall, into the sitting room and to the rear window to once more look out and down at the drop.

He turned sheepishly to a crowd of warm faces in the room and smiled back into their laughter.

**War News!**

- German v-2 rockets start to land in London.
- German army surrenders Marseille to units of invading Allied army, after the landings in the south of France

# 5. Night out on the Town!

"Where are we going?" he asked, after her tossed-over-the-shoulder remark, going up the stairs two at a time, when they'd finished their evening meal.

She halted half way up the flight to turn and smile down at him.

"Fair…fun fair – down by the station!" she repeated, face flushed and excited at the prospect.

"Oh, ah…when?"

"Right now! After I've changed. You wanna go, don't you?"

"'Course!" He grinned back.

They could hear loud music and grinding sounds from the open-air Fun Fair long before they discovered it. The hurdy-gurdy, piped musical sound, clashing with popular record numbers played from gramophone records, the sounds blurted out from lamp-post attached speakers.

With the day light fading, the sudden appearance of Collins' Fun Fair clustered layout of bright and blinking electric light bulbs, revealing waltzers, flying chairs, side show attractions and other tented amusement arcades, was a wonderland of excitement to his young eyes, as they turned the corner of the road onto the site.

Blitz regulations had taken a back seat, now that the German air raids had long since ended, and the war was turning in the Allies favour.

"Well?" she queried, her eyes glistening wide-eyed with active intensity.

"Yeah – like it!" he laughed in response.

They walked into and mingled with the crowds of animated and chattering humanity around the show ground, all intent on a good night out. Tugging on his hand, she led and pulled him with her on to various fun-filled and hair-raising rides. At three pence (1–1/4p) per ride, it was well-worth the outlay, surrounded as they were by eardrum-blasting blaring music and the screams of thrilled riders, thoroughly enjoying the scariness of the experience.

Soon, they were talking and chattering with local youngsters and teenagers they didn't know, but in such an intimate way that outsiders would conclude they'd known each other for yonks!

Questions asked and answers freely given in between laughter, high jinks and humorous outbursts, making for a jolly period of exchanges. It came as natural, making strangers they'd just met into close friends in the flicker of animated rapturous absurdities.

This intense fun-making began to change, as it became apparent that two of the young male teenagers with flattened back short hair styles, wanted Vee to join them for a spot of fun? – without her 'brother' in tow. He realised, amusingly, that she must've ID'd his presence as being her young brother. Well, that was curious, but okay, he mused.

However, Vee managed to take his wrist and yanked him up and onto a nearby ride. Didn't need to be asked twice, because he wanted to ride EVERYTHING.

Once together, in a two-seater section, she turned quickly to him and said that as soon as the ride stopped, he was to get off with her, but on the opposite side to where the two teenagers were conferring privately, between sniggers of mischievousness.

So when the ride slowed to a halt, Vee jerked him up out of the seat as the opportunity arose, dragging him across the wood-slatted platform surround, down the steps and onto the dusty showground; then getting off to a scrambling, twisting run between sections of the crowd, heading for the empty fringes of the Fun Fair.

"Run!" she urged him in a shout, but still holding tightly onto his wrist.

"Why – uh?" he tried questioningly.

"Just RUN!" she ordered, now on empty pavements back around the corner of the road they'd previously travelled down, and out of the area.

Ten minutes later, they fell in through the front door of the house they were staying at.

"Phew!" Vee said, laughing nervously.

"Why did we have to leave so early and in such a hurry?" he managed to gasp.

"Those lads back there were up to no good."

He frowned back at her, naively.

"Trust me," she told him.

"'Kay!" he said, accepting.

After the previous night's shenanigans, excitement during the fright-n'-flight, it was a day down on the beach – or would've been – leastways, had it not rained.

Vee suggested a trip to the pictures, for the early show, which sounded like a good idea, because he was a picture-house fan from way back. These architectural edifices were his favourite havens and haunts for escapism. Having said that, he was a tad coy about what was being shown. Like most boys of his age, categories that attracted his attention – their attention? – and interests, varied, but on the whole centred on westerns, war, thrillers, comedy and sci-fi, but no – and a big NO – to sloppy soppy love and passionate melodramas!

"Your wanna go?" Vee asked.

Cautiously, he probed. "What kinda film?"

"Oh, you'll like it," she cooed, being persuasive.

"How d'you know?" he quietly asked, suspiciously.

"There's a murder in it."

"Yeah? An 'A' picture?"

She nodded. "Ginger Rogers is an American reporter who confesses to killin' somebody."

"What's it called – this picture?"

"*ROXY HART*. Wanna go?"

A quick reflection made him realise it was Saturday night. Back home, he always tried to get out to the pictures, 'cause – well, Saturday night was special. Something to look forward to through-out the week. Not going to the local flea-pit, meant he'd wasted a valuable night out. It was important to use up a Saturday night by going to see and enjoying a good flick. Wouldn't be the same without it. So…

"'Course!" he quickly replied.

Plus, he always liked discovering a new strange cinema, and this visit was no different. Great name, too: Cosy Picture House, Colwyn Bay. Although, there were some boring scenes during the show, on the whole it was a fast-moving racy flick. The cinema building, reminded him – and had a similarity with – another picture house with the same name, in Liverpool. Had the same set up, where patrons entered the small auditorium under the screen, from the entrance. This was something he'd share with his pals, when he got back to September Road, after the weekend away.

**War News!**

- Advancing American armoured units (4th Armoured Division) enter and liberate the French city of Rennes

# 6. Love Is in the Air...Not!

Vee, who was his brother's girlfriend, leastways, they were supposed to be walking out together or something soppy, like that? He'd overheard grown-ups associate the term with naivety, reference to teenagers or the word romantic, which had no place in his vocabulary or understanding of something loosely referred to as socialising between the sexes, whatever that was supposed to be or mean, he reasoned cynically?

Very unnecessarily complicated, for a twelve-year-old to understand.

He found this difficult and made him uneasy, if only because it was not something his young mind could comprehend, handle or discern. Most of his mental coherence of life which flowed around him, was focussed through 'see-at-a-glance' recognition.

Simplified problems.

Made life – easier.

He liked the idea of being sent on a message to Vee's, because her mother – Mrs Sherry – and he knew that wasn't her real name but served its purpose with him, was a real nice adult. She seemed always to genuinely be pleased to see him, even when he turned up unexpectedly. She'd make a fuss of him, i.e. cup of hot cocoa and a biscuit from a square painted-on-flower-decorated metal biscuit tin. Not only that, but it gave him the opportunity to catch up with Marjorie, the girl next door to her – a neighbour's daughter of his same age – who had taken a shine to him, or so it pleased him to imagine so?

She had long blond hair and attractive, lively blue eyes. When she talked, she gushed words and he had difficulty breaking into their conversation to let her know what he thought about this-n'-that, even though he was always being accused of having the gift-of-the-gab. Or, as some would say – less flatteringly – gobby.

Her vivaciousness and outgoing liveliness won his attention, like no other, and as a result he became very attracted to her. He was sure, by her reactions to him, that she knew this. Only thing was, he got the feeling her dad, when the odd occasion arose that he met him by accident, wasn't so forthcoming Probably, because he didn't appear that friendly, like he never smiled his acknowledgement of his presence, especially if he happened – through invitation from Marjorie – to step across the divide fence into their back garden.

In fact, once or twice, he caught her dad looking out from the lounge window into the garden, where he was sat on their lawn chatting to her, with a serious stare, not quite a frown, but looking decidedly unhappy about something? Maybe, it occurred to him, perhaps unfairly, that he didn't trust him getting too chummy with his pretty daughter?

Wasn't for the want of trying, that he didn't get the nod of acceptability from her father. There was a persistent coolness. Couldn't put his finger on it, just sensed it, all the same. He had noticed that when he was chatting to her, and her dad stepped out into the yard, she'd momentarily pause in her conversation and even change the topic, stilted and distanced in the tone of her voice, that is until he returned indoors and their chat couldn't be overheard.

Got so, that a little later – few days, maybe – when he'd cross the fence to have a friendly chat, her father emerged in a bit of a tizz with her over something, and her flippant answers to his requests inflamed him and he stormed up to her and began loudly scolding her in front of him and in no uncertain terms!

He had stepped away – taken-aback, perplexed and embarrassed, especially when he ordered her indoors, and she was forced to obey, only glancing sorrowfully and briefly in his direction, before vacating the yard to do as he bade her, her father following behind. The back door was slammed shut, without a word of apology or even a parting glance.

He heard more shouting inside the house and Marge's voice screaming back recriminations.

All very disturbing. He knew it couldn't be something he'd said, because they hadn't even exchanged pleasantries. Why he should dismiss his socialising with Marge, was a mystery to him? True to say, her father was intent on discouraging their friendship from developing any further, and without his knowing why.

Several days later, on visits to Mrs Sherry's, he'd loitered in the back garden, pretending to examine flowers, but no sign of Margie.

Clearly, her father didn't like him, and so there was nothing he could do about that, 'cepting that he didn't get to have those friendly warm chats with her, anymore. Conversations he'd looked forward to, because she'd always showed an interest in everything and anything he raised as topics, which they might discuss and laugh about together, like school chums they each did not know personally, but were prepared on verbal description to accept, events and incidents during each's recent school day, that is – whenever he got a word in edgeways? Young people's chat was of no interest to adults or grown-ups, which perplexed him still further and all the more, because it was so innocuous – harmless?

He decided to leave off trying to see her, simply because he ran out of ideas and reasons for visiting Mrs Sherry's place, and if he continued to turn up for no reason, they would quickly guess his interest and intent, and he found that thought sensitive to live with and totally embarrassing.

So, it was a couple/three weeks before he rode up on his two-wheeler, really his brother's bike, on a legitimate errand for his mum for Mrs Sherry, to do with – he knew not what?

After pleasantries, he stepped out into the garden, give himself the opportunity to look across at the next-door neighbours windows, in the hope – or just in case – he could catch a glimpse of a blond-haired face with vivid blue eyes, but no, he didn't. He let his eyes wander and roam around to find himself staring at Mrs Sherry, who was stood inside the house and looking out through her back kitchen window. As it so happened, directly at him. Startled by the realisation, he pretended not to notice and instead stared at a starling perched on the fence.

The back door swung inwards and Mrs Sherry's smiling face appeared.

"You looking for Marjorie?"

"Marjorie?" he responded innocently, as though that subject was far removed from his mind.

"Saw you looking across the fence for her?"

"Oh…" he said giving her a prepared and vacant look. And to emphasise his point, shook his head, again, as though no such thought had entered his head or was likely to?

"Well, if you are, I just saw her walking down the road."

"Oh, well…might as well say 'hello'," he allowed, stepping quickly to the side of the house and a flagged path, which led to the road at the front.

"Thought you might!" he heard Mrs Sherry say as he passed her face filled with a knowing beam.

With effort, he managed not to match her smile and even deliberately slowed his stride, to hide a keenness on his behalf.

Out in the road, Marge was nowhere to be seen. He trotted down the road to where there was a bend. As he followed the bend, she came into his line of vision and he slowed, because she was in the company of other kids their age. It wasn't something he was prepared for and Mrs Sherry had failed to add on this snippet of information.

He was disappointed and a tad annoyed to see she was surrounded by others, and he couldn't sneak up and surprise her, as he'd planned to do, without being spotted by her beforehand.

He was within a dozen yards of her when he was seen approaching by another girl, who instantly nudged Marge and snickered, mouthing some nothingness into her shell-like. Marge immediately turned and showed genuine pleasure at his appearance.

By this time he joined the throng.

Marge's girl companion, stepped forward and placed herself between her and a tall blond-haired boy of similar age, gripping the forearm of this tall gangly youth and tugging him forward.

She announced loudly and displaying a devious and artful smile, introducing the curly-haired lad. "This is Marjorie's new boy-friend, Pringle!" she said, enjoying the effect it had on the sudden visitor in their midst.

**War News!**

- After many days of bitter and bloody fighting against the cream of German Panzer Divisions defending the line in Western France, British troops have broken through the stubborn enemy defence lines around Caen to enter and liberate the city.

# 7. A-Sailing We Will Go

Part of growing up is trying different things to do. Like tree-climbing, which is a great sport and a test of a boy's ambition, challenge and physical attributes – fun, too. There were, unfortunately, only so many trees around to climb in a city suburb, compared to what they might find in the countryside, especially where he was earlier evacuated to. The problem about climbing trees around Anfield was the continual harassment by adults, busy-bodies and nosey-pokes sticking their noses in where it didn't belong, followed by boring verbal utterances, like:

- 'What are you doing up there?'
- 'You shouldn't be up there in that tree!'
- 'Get down out of there, before you hurt yourself!'
- 'You're gonna break your bloody neck if yous fall out of there!'
- 'Does yer mother know, you're up there?'

Most times, it's got nothing to do with them, just that some grown-ups like think they always know best, and to his way of thinking, they don't – not alwus, that is.

Which brought him around to seeking other interests. The end of the school hols was rapidly approaching, which meant they were all herded back to the drudgery of regular Monday-to-Friday School Days, class room discipline and boring homework. So he knew he'd best get a move on and not waste another day, sitting like a bunch of crows on an old wall with the other kids, and doing sweet nothings, wastin' away their valuable freedoms and all-day do-as-you-want.

"They've got row boats on Newsham Park, lads, I've heard. Any of you lot tried them out?"

The sun came out from behind rain clouds and promised to shine.

There was an immediate awakening and raising of heads as the idea touched-lit and suddenly ignited their grey matter.

"Yeah, that's right," said one brightly, jerking upright.

"How much?" asked another, pragmatically as always, this being the first question that accompanied an excursion.

"Coppers," he said, not at all sure, but knowing that Liverpool City Council couldn't charge too much or it would deter the punters.

"Let's go?" agreed at least three brave souls. Some kept mum, not happy about deep water with a built-in notion that if God meant them to venture there, he'd have furnished everyone with flippers for arms and gills on either side of their necks. Grave suspicions of a watery grave, prevented any significant support for the idea.

The quartet arrived at the edge of the lake and made their way down steps onto the floating platform and pay-point, where a collection of vacant narrow four/five-seater row boats with a pair of oars pulled inboard each, were moored. An elderly park keeper attendant was leaned up against the cabin pay-point and watched their approach with a jaundiced eye, while he smoked his woody and scowled in their direction, probably because – the kids reckoned – they weren't accompanied by an adult.

"How old are you?" the old man asked.

Knowing full-well he had to be fourteen or thereabouts to be allowed and trusted to rent out a row boat, he quickly, smoothly and confidently lied that he was, and that they all were! The fact that there wasn't one of them over thirteen, was neither here nor there, as far as he was concerned. Even the attendant wasn't really that bothered if the truth be known. The important fact was, that he'd asked them their ages and this had been witnessed by the young teenaged girl cashier chewing gum and looking bored-to-death, inside a wood cabin structure, behind a small window aperture.

The aged attendant gave them a baleful questioning glance, before shrugging and nodded to the teenage girl assistant in the cabin, to whom they passed their money.

"Listen," the elderly attendant said to them, coughing his lungs up as he did so, "half an hour, okay?"

He led them to two wood row boats tied up to a mooring ring, then raised a hand to halt them. He didn't enquire if they possessed a watch between them, because he knew kids couldn't afford such luxuries.

"Listen," the old park keeper said again. "When I shouts 'TIME', yous to come in. Do it right away, okay?"

The four innocent heads, tight-lipped, nodded obediently, but smirking between them.

He led his pals into the first boat, lifting and slipping each oar carefully into the oar holders and then dipping the widest section into the lake water on each side. He looked up to his partner who clambered awkwardly into the stern and grinned at him with pleasure.

"Push us off!" he ordered from his rowing position.

"Don't you mean, 'cast off'?" his shipmate corrected, with a matching grin.

"Whatever?" he retorted.

"Yessir, cap'n!" was the crisp response.

They managed quite well to draw away from the mooring and toward the centre of the lake, the oars squeaking and creaking in their holders. Their other two mates, in their boat, decided on a different approach, sitting side-by-side, handling an oar each. The attendant gave their boat a push start, but they only managed to row in a circle, because they hadn't thought about nor mastered coordinating their strokes, and not only that, but because of their clumsiness, an oar bounced out of the oar holder and slipped from the grasp of one of the boys. It plopped onto the placid surface with a slight splash. The lad who'd lost control, couldn't grab hold of it, but did manage to almost tip the boat over as he threw his weight onto the gunwale leaning out, but was saved in time as his mate made a grab at part of his jersey to save him from plunging in after the oar. The boat rocked violently, but then as they froze, settled itself.

"Hey!" the boy who'd lost the oar, yelled in concern.

The oar drifted away…

He was pulling firmly on his oars and into the lake, when he saw over the shoulder of his partner, the pretty pickle their mates were making in the second row boat.

"Don't fret, we're comin' to rescue yoos!" shouted his partner from the stern, waving both arms and nearly toppling over the side himself, from laughter.

He pulled in an oar and used the other to send their boat in a circle and nosed his craft back to help rescue the loose oar, which was adrift and now about five feet from the other boat.

The plight of their mates gifted and provided a great deal of further excited nervous laughter on their part.

Back on the mooring platform, the elderly attendant scowled across the water in their direction in unconcealed disgust.

"Get us our oar!" the boys in difficulty shouted to their mates.

"We're coming, you blind?" He laughed, controlling himself. To his partner, he shouted. "Lean over and grab that oar as I come alongside it – and, no – don't stand up over the side or we'll both be swimming for it."

"No, I ain't that daft," partner grinned back, leaning over the side and watching as their boat manoeuvred and came about to retrieve the loose oar adrift on the lake's surface.

This retrieval was carefully and successfully accomplished and after more manoeuvring, they swung in close to their mate's boat and gently raised the handed end of it to one of the lads, who this time, remained seated and dragged the dripping wet oar up and over the gunwale, slipped it – with clumsy difficulty, puffing and blowing in his efforts – to slide the oar back into place in the swivel holder, before once more dipping the blade back into the water.

"Phew!" the boy managed, smiling self-consciously, but thankful.

"Try not to lose your oar out of the rowlock, 'kay," he shouted toward the clumsy pair, nodding, waiting for their confirmation.

They hovered at a short distance away, in case the second boat encountered additional difficulty, before deciding they were a-okay and pulled away firmly.

"You done this before?" partner asked.

"Yeah, great fun, isn't it? Trick is, not to stand up, unbalance the boat or – lose an oar."

"Yer-right!" partner repeated, laughing. "Lose an oar!"

With their mates now in anxious command of their craft, they pulled further away and under one of the foot bridges into another secluded section of lake.

"Heave away, me hearties!" said partner in the spirit of Treasure island's 'Long John Silver', clearly enjoying himself. "D'you think our troops used these kind of boats to invade on D-Day?"

"No chance!" he replied, bursting into cackling laughter. "They had those LST's, but 'course, in Nelson's time, they had long boats and cutters with oars."

Their row boat turned a bend and disturbed a raft of ducks, who scattered out of their way and to the safety of empty reaches, uttering loud harsh squawking as they splashed in fright and perhaps anger?

"Wonder how deep this lake is?" he said, more to himself than partner, pulling aboard both oars, staring over the side and peering closely into the muddied depths. He lifted an oat into vertical position and probed the lake bed. Was immediately surprised as the blade encountered the muddy bottom after only penetrating three feet down.

"Wow. I thought it was deeper than this?" he commented.

"Probably, so'as we don't drown ourselves, most likely," partner giggled.

"Think you're right. Anyway, your turn to row, 'kay?" he said, as he placed each oar back in the holders and rowed toward the nearest grassy bank. He let the boat run into the reeds and mud; then jumped out onto the bank, turned, squatted down to hold the gunwale, while partner stepped into the rower's position and fussed until comfortable. He stepped across the edge of the boat and took up the position in the stern.

His mate, between the oars, leaned out sideways and shoved away at the bank, to send the craft back out onto the lake again. Sat in the rower's seat and confident, partner allowed the oars to dip into the water and rowed slowly, but firmly, back into the centre of the lake.

In the distance, he caught sight of their mates, still only just about to row under the bridge, using the oars to clip the surface, causing showers of water to cascade, but hardly enabling them to make much progress. Nevertheless, they were clearly enjoying themselves, too, and pretty soon both boats met up, or rather, they succeeded in colliding together and getting the oars jammed or entangled against and between each other's boat. They then engaged in applying handfuls of lake water hurled airborne in each other's directing in a flurry of splashing and mayhem, adding much to their excitement, drenching each other and at the same time managing to raise the water level in the bottom of their boats. This melee upset other people who were sedately rowing nearby on the lake. Scolding remarks were uttered in their direction.

Wasn't long before their half hour was up and the elderly attendant on the float platform began throwing a fit at their wayward ways, waving his arms over his head, pointing at them and shouting fit to burst, face purple with indignation.

The boys, of course, pretended not to notice.

Adults in nearly boats who had complained at their antics, killjoys – all of them – began pointing to the attendant's call for their return. They couldn't properly ignore the attentions they were receiving for ever, and reluctantly allowed their recall to be acknowledged, knowing full-well that if they caused any more bother, they might be refused the opportunity to go boating at some future date, especially if the elderly park keeper was in attendance.

**War News!**

- RAF bombers and fighters attack transportation and airfield targets in Northern France, destroying facilities, rail-links and Luftwaffe aircraft on the ground.
- Florence is liberated by units of British and South African army divisions.

# 8. Foes to Be Avoided

After the sea battle of Lake Newsham, walking away from the boating lake was an anti-climax. They drifted along the park paths, having exhausted the memories of remembering their recent water-bash, each in his own thoughts, kicking loose stones as the opportunity availed itself.

"We goin' back to our road?" one lone voice asked, laden with boredom.

"Might as well," supplied another of the quartet.

"Let's go back along Lister Drive and follow the road over the railway and down to Green Lane, and then on to Tuebrook?" he interrupted.

"Why?" said an another, with knitted bows, wanting to know.

"Because," he replied, narked by the question.

"Because what?" knitted brow persevered, nipping quickly out in front and ahead of them to turn and confront him.

Without stopping and stepping around his inquisitor to continue, said. "Because, it's a different way to go home."

"We don't have any money to go to the pictures?"

"Did I say that?"

"No, but the on'y reason we go down Green Lane is to go to the Carlton Picture House."

"I didn't even mention the Carlton," he said adamantly.

"Well, that's what I thought you were talking about?"

"How could we go to the Carlton, when we don't have any money, huh?" he replied, picking up on his antagonist's last comment.

The other, now slipped back to the rear, as they dawdled past the front gate entrance to the Power Station on Lister Drive, reacted. "Keep yer bloody hair on, okay? I on'y thought, yeah?"

This time, he kept his trap shut and tried to calm down and didn't respond further.

Antagoniser said, as they walked up and over the road bridge running across a railway line, to the other two mates. "'E's got a right gob on!"

He decided to ignore the remark and now concentrated on a group of about a dozen kids about their age, walking in their direction towards them, muttering between themselves and staring at the four as they crossed an open stretch of flat land, where he'd seen the German POWs, the last time he came out of the Baths.

The group, at a muttered signal between each other, spread out so that the covered a wide stretch ahead of the quartet, with their flanks starting to come forward and seemed as though they might envelope the four.

At about a dozen feet or so, he stopped and held the other three back. The larger gang confronted the quartet. He had, by now, recognised a confrontation when he saw one.

"Where you goin'?" the ringleader in the centre of the approaching line gruffly demanded.

"Just walking through to Green Lane," he replied for the quartet.

"I never see yoos, before?" ringleader accused.

"Likewise," he replied.

"You tryin' to be funny?"

"Why d'you want to know?"

"I'm askin' the questions, not you," ringleader frowned.

"So, what d'you want from us?"

"You're not from around here?"

"We're just walkin' through to Green Lane."

"RICHIE!" ringleader shouted out, without turning his head or altering his gaze.

A young kid of about eight, pushed his way forward from behind their line and up to where ringleader stood, the gang behind him inching closer and around the quartet in a threatening half circle.

"Dese the punks who kicked yuh?" ringleader questioned, out of the side of his mouth.

The quartet stared down at the sharp-eyed youngster as he gave them a close once-over.

"Well?"

"Not sure?" the kid muttered.

"Where you lot from?" ringleader quizzed.

"September Road – it's off Lower Breck Road."

There was a pause while this sunk in. Ringleader looked down at the staring youngster stood alongside him. "You said, they was from Prescot Road?"

"Old Swan-ites," the eight-year-old said, looking up, and then eyed the quartet coldly.

"We okay to go, now?" he asked their leader as his three mates closed in behind him.

"Fuck off back the way you came!" ringleader barked.

"You got no argument with us," he defended.

"Maybe, we just don't like your bloody faces?"

He knew where this line of chat was headed, as ringleader – he figured out – had decided he had something to prove and with enough numbers to back him up, could push his aggressiveness. He could have repeated the same retort, back to him, but could see that kind of remark was all they needed as an excuse to start something.

"Okay," he said, lightly. "We'll go back the way we came," and turning said to the other three. "Okay, lads, let's go back."

This remark gained precious seconds for him to lead and turn the quartet around to head back toward the bend in the road across the bridge and return to Newsham Park.

"RUN FOR IT!" he suddenly shouted to the other three, who needed no bidding to follow in a dashing sprint for the road bridge bend, ahead of them.

The gang were not prepared for the quartet's hurried departure and wasted more valuable seconds waiting for their leader to give the word to give chase.

"LET'S GET DEM!" ringleader finally yelled, by now the quartet were thirty feet away and legging it.

He raced slightly ahead of his three compatriots to where the road doglegged over the rail bridge.

"There's a platform on the other side of the wall – so they won't see us," he said, waving and beckoning frantically with the knowledge of having seen it previously used by workmen, and with a wood ladder attached, which descended down to the trees-n'-bushes at the edge of Newsham Park, itself.

He leaped up and over the stone wall at the side of the road, which now sloped down into the park. He dropped onto the eight-foot-wide wood platform, twenty feet above ground level, as the others scrambled over and followed him.

"What now?" a mate shrilled.

"Down the ladder," he told them quickly.

"What ladder?" his mate's voice now a frightened shriek.

Something was terribly wrong!

As they clumped together on the platform, he looked frenziedly around for the ladder and safe escape, but it had been removed.

A cry above them, on the wall, focussed their attention, as a face appeared and shouted. "HERE DE ARE!"

His three mates turned to him in horror.

They were trapped.

Stones would come hurtling down on them, within seconds.

He glanced in trepidation over the edge of the platform, and at the same time heard the gleeful yells from the road above them, converging in loud running heavy steps and whoops of blood-curdling joy.

"Nothing for us – JUMP!" he yelled, leading the way in a suicidal leap into eternity…

He wasn't alone, as the other three tumbled after him in terror, but fortunately crashing down onto a load of thickets, shrubs and other tightly hedged in bushes, which broke their fall, 'cepting from numerous scratches and grazes on knees, legs, arms and legs.

There was the shock of coming to an abrupt, cushioned and body rattling stop on mother earth, but apart from the shock of the fall, some painful ankles, raw-skinned abrasions and sore knee-joints, there were fortunately no broken bones, as they picked themselves up, extracted themselves from the bushes, hobbled and stumbled, breathing hard, away as fast as they could into the safety of the Newsham Park, with only the yelled threats from the platform on the top of the wall, ringing in their ears.

"WE'SE'LL GET CHEW, NEXT TIME!" shouted after them, but no serious hot pursuit.

### War News!

- Warsaw uprising has become a bloody confrontation between ill-equipped, but spirited resistance fighters, and entrenched well-armed German troops. Uprising was only planned to last for several days to give the nearby Russian forces chance to enter the city and relieve them. However, puzzlingly, the Soviets had halted their advance and dug-in on their side of the river.

## 9. The Big Stick

It was finally, the first day back at school after the summer hols. Months of previous school discipline had disappeared during the long break and replaced with genuine ebullient enthusiastic youthful exuberance, and an open and improved interest in what each others got up to during that time? It was a moment of coming together for those who only saw each other during school hours. There were happy stories to tell, like the trip to Leeswood and the water-battle on Newsham Park lake later confrontation with 'two-legged animals' from Lister Drive and Green Lane.

There were the sad admissions of fathers or elder brothers reportedly killed or missing during or after military missions against opposing forces of the Axis powers. Although the Allies were reportedly winning the war, there were the inevitable tragic casualties and loss of loved ones on foreign fields, and the subsequent pain and anguish that this entailed in families living apart due to the war, not to mention the financial stress and burdens experienced by mums.

However, most of the hardship and effects of the war were shouldered by mums-n'-dads, so school kids were to some extent protected from the dreadful spin-offs, even though they were nonetheless aware of the inevitable consequences.

From Big Brother's letters home to Mum and Dad, he learned that he'd been moved from his southern army station on Salisbury Plain, over and into Europe, somewhere in Belgium.

Because it was the first day back at school, the teachers, most of whom were brought out of retirement, were inclined to be a tad testy and short tempered, which didn't go unnoticed by the class, who relished the thought of making their teaching day more difficult than it normally was, and of special interest and a mischievous challenge, so the class – not all, of course – just the dissatisfied and restless malcontents would seize any situation that could be exploited to their own ends.

He settled down as the aged male teacher began to read from his prepared notes and opening review of the lesson subject, so far.

His attention was diverted from the dreary monotone of tutor's utterance to a picture postcard thrust into his open hand from a nearby classmate. It was the usual type of seaside item, which can be found on a rack of similar light-hearted humoresque cartoons, some of which, like the one in the palm of his hand. A beach-side backdrop and a middle-aged woman of gargantuan proportions, wearing a tight – too small-lady's swimming costume with a gas mask covering her face and wearing a paper hat atop of her bright red hair reading 'KISS ME QUICK!' stood facing a short little man with a moustache of similar age, a white handkerchief protecting his bald pate, but still in his long-sleeved shirt, braces over his shoulders and pant bottoms turned up to his knees to save them from getting wet, as the tide crept in. He is staring dubiously up at the lady's head, his forefinger pressed against closed lips, above a caption on the bottom of the postcard, reading 'What happened next?'

He held the card between his fingers and turned to stare at the boy sat next to him, who wore a wide-mouthed grin and at that moment leaned forward and whispered a rude comment in his shell-like with a trumpeting snort of uncontrollable laughter.

Unfortunately, as he held the item, the elderly teacher heard the noise and glanced up in time to see him, postcard in hand, and head turned away seemingly to engage in the hilarity.

"You boy – whatever your name is?" Teach spluttered in a surge of short temper.

Card still in his hand, he turned back to face the speaker from the front of the class, but taken aback, when he saw the teacher frowning in his direction.

"What have you got there? Let us all have a look at what you think is more important than your education?"

He was momentarily struck dumb.

"C'mon," teacher spoke up crustily. "Come up here and bring whatever it is in your hand, you're showing to your cronies…"

He sat perfectly still, mortified, unsure of where this was going?

"I SAID," teacher, now irate, "bring yourself up here – NOW!"

He heard a couple of muffled giggles either side of him, as he stood to his feet and walked forward up the aisle to the front of the class, and to where the teacher was standing, the postcard still in his hand.

The tutor reached and tore the postcard from his fingers and perused the cartoon. His anger could be seen building in the frown on his face.

"This boy," he said pointing at him, "hopes to get a job when he leaves school, but the only job he's likely to get is selling dirty postcards on street corners!"

The class took this to be a signal for loud communal laughter as the tutor turned his irate attention back to the boy next to him; then reached under his desk and pulled out a bamboo cane.

"Your impudence will be punished!" teacher said, poking the cane under the boy's right hand and raising it to waist level, his back to the class.

The teacher pulled the cane away and then raised it in the air.

He stared back at the teacher's angry features.

He couldn't believe this was happening?

The tutor had got it all wrong, but there was no way he could protest his innocence. As he was facing the whole class, his vision sought out the perp who'd instigated all of this.

*WHACK!*

The cane thrashed down across his inside extended fingers and the pain shot through his wrist joint and up his right arm like an electric shock. He stared down at the ugly red welt starting to form across the palm his open hand.

He made the instant mistake of glowering back at the class and saw of group of his mates all pulling the most atrocious ugly cynical, but comical, faces in his direction, which couldn't be seen by teacher, they knew.

As humour is contagious, they also knew they'd get a reaction from him, who was being chastised, if unfairly. He lost it and couldn't prevent himself from a short giggle surging out of him in response.

"It's funny? – Funny?" the tutor snapped, not able to see the section of class making faces at the boy before him.

*WHACK!*

"Does that calm your jocularity? – Huh?" he barked in rage.

As he walked back to his place, holding one hand in the other, he gave the classmate, who'd involved him in all of this, a murderous glare – a look of intended revenge.

### War News!

- Unsuccessful assassination on Adolf Hitler whilst the German Fuhrer was visiting German Army Headquarters in Rastenburg, East Prussia, has been reported to the world press.

# 10. An Unpleasant Incident!

He finished reading last night's Liverpool Echo, but his thoughts returned to the front page and the cinema index, highlighting the current films being shown. This was really the only page he was interested in, plus the War headlines on the back page, together with maps that were always connected to the main story, showing with black arrows, just how far the Allied armies had penetrated across France and how far they had pushed the German armies away from the coast, in so doing.

Back on the first page, his eyes stared down at the cinema index and narrowed on one of the films being shown, which was a pirate swashbuckler *The Black Swan*, starring Tyrone Power, who he'd once seen in a film, still vivid in his memory, as a matador in *Blood and Sand*. He certainly wasn't interested in the love and competitive passion between first Linda Darnell and then Rita Heyworth, but the scenes in the bullring and the matador being gored, were still very clear in his mind.

This time, Tyrone Power was a sword-fencing adventurer in the Caribbean during the time of Pirates with red-bearded George Sanders and Sir Henry Morgan as the governor of

Jamaica played by Laird Cregar. 'Course, there had to be a woman in the film, and that was the spirited Maureen O'Hara.

He, and one of his friends, caught a tram on Rocky Lane in the Anfield district of the city, and alighted at the top end of West Derby Road, where the cinema was situated, for the afternoon matinee performance.

Once inside and seated in the middle stalls, the performance began and as the film reeled-off, proved and lived-up to all the exciting scenes and sequences they'd already heard about and approvingly expected of it.

Half way through the film, he was conscious of an intrusion of feeling on his left leg. Wasn't his friend adjusting his position on the seat next to him, because he was sat on his right side. No, this feeling was from his left. He glanced sideways and noticed in the darkness, a middle-aged man in a long raincoat, staring and focussed up at the screen. Deciding to give the stranger the benefit of the doubt, used his own left hand to sweep the intruding fingers off his left leg, and turned back to concentrate on screen as events in the story unfolded.

Couple of minutes later, he felt those same fingers intruding on his left leg, yet again, and this time was incensed at the insulting and cheeky action. There was no doubt now, that this elderly man was intent on a disgusting and unpleasant act, and He was the targeted victim.

"My big brother is joining me an' my mate in a few minutes, an' I'm gonna tell him about you!" he half shouted in a shocked voice.

Instantly, this outburst caused several adult heads – mostly ladies in the audience – to turn abruptly in their direction, some hissing "Hush!"

The elderly stranger immediately raised up off his seat and made a hasty move along the row toward the aisle.

"Who are you talkin to?" his mate, suddenly concerned, asked, bending and leaning forward to look across him in time to see the back of the fast receding elderly man in a long coat, pressing a dark trilby into place on top of a mop of untidy grey hair, now at the aisle and walking quickly up it toward the exit from the stalls.

"That old man put his hand on my leg!" he whispered earnestly, still anxious.

"The old fellah? – What did you say?"

He repeated what he'd said to the old man.

"Your bother? Is he coming here?" his mate's surprised voice responded.

"No! No, you fool! I had to say something' and it was the only thing I could think of!"

A soldier with his arm around his girlfriend, and sat in front of them, turned abruptly.

"Will yoos two – SHUD-UP!" he growled, as his young lady's face also twisted around, scowling and frowning hard.

A torch-light flashed in their direction along the row and they were instantly caught in the beam and startled by it.

"Ay!" said a burly figure in cinema uniform. "If yoos don't behave yourselves, I'll throw the two of yoos out!" his low gruff voice threatened.

"It was that man!" he responded, pointing over and across the seats toward the back of the stalls.

More heads turned around in their seats to look annoyed and vexed that their interest in the film was continually being disturbed.

"Come out here!" the cinema attendant demanded, with an impatient wave of his hand, the torch now switched off.

The two of them left their seats quickly, but reluctantly, and threaded their way along the row to the aisle to join the waiting attendant who then hustled them up the aisle, out of the stalls, through swing doors and into the emptiness of the lobby of the cinema.

"What's all that bother yous two were getting up to?" the big man in the uniform of an admiral of a South American Navy demanded, glowering his annoyance at them.

He told the uniformed man. His mate interrupted to confirm he'd seen the stranger scurrying off.

"Why didn't chew come and tell me?"

He argued that there wasn't time, and it all happened so quickly.

"Alright! Alright! If yoos see this dirty old bugger again, come and tell me, an' I'll grab him by the scruff of his neck and throw him out. Okay?"

They silently nodded their agreement.

"Now, yoos can go back in to watch the rest of the filem, but not in them same seats or people'll be complaining' again. Go sit some where's else, yeah?"

Later, after leaving the Picture House they caught a tram heading home, and scampered up the stairs to the top deck – at the front, of course – and began discussing the disturbing invasion of his privacy. At first serious, but then his mate told him about his auntie who had experienced something similar at the Empress, in Tuebrook. So, the next time she went there, his mate went on to tell, she took a long hat-pin with her concealed in her handbag.

"The very next time?" he asked his mate.

"Well, not exactly the very next time, but – anyway, let me tell the story…"

"Okay."

"Seems this fellah…"

"Was he an old man?"

"Will you wait a minute! Let me tell you what happened!" his mate steamed, annoyed at his interruption.

"'Kay."

"When he put his hand on her leg, she slid her hand into her bag and pulled the hat-pin out and drove it down hard into his arm…" his mate, telling the story, was now unable to control his laugh. "An' this fellah leaps up off his seat an' screams like a woman…" His laughter now knowing no bounds. "An' the whole row knew what it was this fellah had done, an' as he left his seat to rush away, everybody in that row gave him a punch as his squeezed past them!"

"Go way, – really?"

"If their husbands had of been there," his mate continued, "they'd 'ave given 'im a bloody good hiding!"

"Serves him right!" he agreed.

"That's what should happen to that ole fellah, that touched your leg."

"Yeah, that's right."

"'Course if he had a hiding off some of our dads, he wouldn't go touching other kids, like he did you."

"Police would lock him up," he interrupted.

His pal shook his head. "Don't need no police for that. Ordinary dads could sort his type out. Listen, he wouldn't do it again. Leastways, he'd think twice about tryin' it, 'cause fellahs like him are more scared of our dads and grown-up brothers, than being arrested by the police."

"Yep. Get bashed up. Getting' his just deserts!"

"My dad sez, if these fellahs who do that with kids got a good bashin', they'd be too afraid to try it again."

"Soon shot out of his seat in a hurry!"

"Maybe, he believed yuh."

"Believed me?"

"That your big brother was gonna join us in the Pictures?"

Penny dropped. "Oh yeah!"

The two boys fell about giggling and laughing out loud, to the bewilderment of other passengers travelling on the top deck of the No. 12 'Green-Goddess' tram heading down West Derby Road to Rocky Lane.

### War News!

- Battle for Normandy intensifies. German 7th Army (Army Group B) and the Fifth Panzer Army (Panzergruppe West), throw in reserves to hold the Allied onslaught, but are unable to prevent the US Third Army pushing south and then East, with the British and Canadians converging and forming the northern arm

# 11. Sudden End to Piano Lessons

Upon his return to Liverpool with Bro and his little brother, after their great little holiday together in North Wales, a week back back and relived events over the dinner table with Mum-n'-Dad, who – he was pleased to notice – were still all ears to their exploits.

He'd talked, they listened.

They asked questions and replied light-heartedly and flippantly, and he hoped his answers were funny. Must've been because they grinned as he finished.

There was an anti-climax at the end of this happy recall of the week away, when Mum, collecting the dirty dishes to wash in the sink, said – as an afterthought – over her shoulder.

"You'll have missed doing your piano exercises, so tonight you can make up for what you've missed. Oh, and don't forget, you've got an appointment with the piano teacher tomorrow night!"

Missed? He hadn't missed anything!

'Course he'd forgotten about it, but that was different.

*What a pain*, he thought as he came back down to earth with a wallop.

His frown deepened when he realised he couldn't go back out, after tea, to discuss the holiday shenanigans together with bro and all the rest of the boys he hung around with in the road.

He'd been looking forward to that, and there was no way he could wriggle out of the piano exercises. Mum had told him she'd had to pay for that lesson, even though he hadn't attended, because it was through no fault of the piano teacher that he didn't attend his appointment, the previous week. If he became 'difficult', because he wanted to go out, Mum would've been disappointed and hurt, having paid toward his holiday, sent food coupons with money agreed and in a sealed envelope to Mrs Griffiths, plus extra pocket money to spend during the week.

He dragged himself into the front room, sat down on the piano stool, lifted the heavy polished lid up from the keys and began to sort himself out, with which exercises he'd worked on. Then, he commenced to play. His kid's depression soon melted away as he concentrated, eyes reading the notations on the sheet music before him, whilst his fingers sought out the right keys to accompany the printed notes.

Following day, his briefcase containing his exercise sheets, note pad and pencil, was under his arm as he skipped up the stone steps to the music teacher's house on Clifton Road. He had personal misgivings about how things would go, considering his lack of recent practice. Wasn't possible to waffle or dither his way through the lesson, because with piano tuition, pupils could either play it right or they couldn't? There was no way he could 'con' his way through. So, he had forebodings about how it would pan out? Besides, Mum always quizzed him after the lessons.

He knocked, waited and turned his screwed-up eyes to stare up and then down the road.

As nobody answered, he thought for a brief moment, he'd got the day wrong – or Mum had?

Better still, there was nobody at home?

He was about to knock yet again, when he heard somebody on the inside, drawing back or turning the knob of the yale lock.

The door swung back and his eyes met those of a stranger. He flashed a quick glance at the number to check he'd got the right house?

"You here for a piano lesson?" the old lady in her sixties asked, leaning forward to peer through her bi-focal and blinking to adjust her vision of him.

"S'right," he said, mystified at the sight of the unknown stranger, but no – wasn't she the woman who'd answered the door on a previous occasion? Piano teacher's mother, maybe?

"Well, she's in hospital," explained the old lady, which – as horrible as it might sound to adults – was music to his ears.

His spirits soared!

She opened her mouth and continued. He suddenly seriously focussed on what she was saying, 'cause Mum would want to know about this development, and in detail. It wasn't serious, the old lady explained. This greatly diminished his temporary exaltation. She went on to say that her daughter – his piano teacher, so presumably she was her elderly parent – had left the house that morning to go on a message to the shops, when a ladder – the window cleaner was using to wash her windows – slipped through his hands and fell onto and across her head and shoulders. Hospital confirmed it wasn't serious, but they were keeping her in overnight for observation, and that she'd be in touch as soon as she recovered, returned home, and felt well enough to continue teaching music lessons.

He quickly stuttered an appropriate and respectful expression of concern, knowing his mum would ask him what he said in reply, when he learned about the accident?

He was also mindful – originally – at the onset of the lessons, of his mum telling him. "The ability to play the piano, you'll find as you grow up, is a great social asset."

He remained to be convinced.

The door closed behind him as he trotted and skipped lightly down the steps from the front door of the house and out onto the pavement.

*Well*, he thought, *that's a how-d'you-do or surprising development!* He couldn't stop himself smirking at the outcome of events. Still, he reigned himself in, less passing grown-ups catching sight of the silly smirk on his face, might jump to the conclusion or take it to mean he was slightly bonkers or crackers, and to walk on the opposite side of the road, just to be careful and be on the safe side!

**War News!**

- Combined army units of Free French forces and elements of the US Army enter and seize Lyon, as part of the successful Allied advance from the Normandy Beaches.
- German V-2 rockets, part of a new terror weapon devised and invented by German scientists, began dropping on London.

- Elements of the US 1st Marine Division and US Army 81st Infantry Division, combine as part of the amphibious invasion force, landing on the Japanese held small coral island of Peleliu, Palau Islands, in the Pacific.
- Bulgarian capital of Sofia, has been successfully attacked and occupied by the Soviet 3rd Ukrainian Army, throwing the Axis armies into retreat.

# 12. What Did You Do in the War, Dad?

"My dad's in the army," replied one of the lads, leaning and lounging – arms folded – against a hedge in front of the house.

"Doin' what?" asked his mate.

"Er," scratching his head, looking across the road at nothing in particular in order to concentrate on an answer. "In the artillery. Was one of the 'Desert Rats' who chased Rommel all the way out of North Africa."

"Oh, yes!" his mate grinned, enjoying the response.

The friend, they were waiting for, and who was finishing his evening meal, could be heard leaving the house somewhere behind them, dragging the door shut – slamming it too, but hidden from their view by the hedge. They knew he was coming and that he didn't have to go to his piano lessons, that night. Fine, as far as they were concerned – which, they were not. It was just something his mother had decided he ought to do, they'd been told, and they were glad their mothers had never mentioned the subject. One had a piano at home, but the other didn't.

Seemed like to them, and they'd already discussed this business of who had or did not have, an upright piano in their front room at home. Was like some sort of rating: families who owned a piano, like it was the 'in' thing with older families, because it meant they could have a 'knees-up' whenever they had something to celebrate. 'Course, now-a-days, families scaled down, preferring to buy a gramophone. Besides, with the war being on, there were no piano's to be had, 'cepting second-hand ones at extortionate prices. Was kinder on their parents' moneybox, and a whole lot cheaper than buying a 'joanna'. Again, second-hand only. Not only that, but it didn't take up or require as much space – a gramophone, that is.

He came walking quickly down his front path still munching the remains of his dinner, into a masticated, well-chewed morsal of the meal, and found them – silent, for a change – beyond his front garden hedge, but then began to exchange small chat as he appeared on the pavement.

"What you two jawing about?" he queried, as he joined them.

The boy speaking didn't want to mention piano, in case he took the huff, and instead said simply. "Gramophones."

"What about them?"

"Some folks have portables, an'…"

"My mum's got one that's a piece of furniture," he elaborated, still chewing. "It's a wind-up type with a polished lid on the top, and right underneath are two small doors that open for the speaker. The bottom is a big cupboard to hold all her records – storage space. Must be – what?" He paused, while he mentally assessed. "About three-an'-a-half feet high, slim, shiny cabinet. You wouldn't think it was a gramophone until you lifted the lid."

One of the lads, added. "Ours is just a portable."

He swallowed the last piece of his dinner. "'Course, the new ones – yous heard of them, yet?"

"G'won!"

"Electric player. Sound is marvellous – sensational!"

"We was just talkin', really, about our dads being in the army. Your's isn't in any of the Services, right?"

"Too old. When the last call-up came, you had to be fit and under forty-two years old."

"Lucky, then?" re-joined one.

"Not really. He was in the first one."

"What? – The last war?"

"Great war," he corrected.

"How old was yer dad?"

"Eighteen."

There was a pause while they thought about it.

"So, what did your dad do in the war?"

The other boy didn't wait for an answer, but moved himself away from the hedge, bouncing an old tennis ball in front of him and began to edge along the pavement. "Thought we wus gonna have a game of footie?"

The subject of their conversation lapsed and they broke into a half walk, run-n'-dribble, kicking the ball between them as they proceeded up the road.

Later, back home in the kitchen with Mum, who was washing the dinner dishes in the sink and Dad browsing through the pages of the Liverpool Evening Express, he recalled the conversation between his mates. Uppermost and to the fore, was the question: What did your dad do in the war?

"Dad," he began, standing alongside the kitchen table and staring out through the window into the darkness of and early night.

"'Ello?" Dad acknowledged, without lifting his head from the broadsheet he held before him.

"What did you do in the war?"

"Which one? This one or the last?"

"The – er, one you were in? The fourteen-eighteen war?"

"I was in the Lancashire Fusiliers, but you know that already."

"Yeah, that's right, but some of the things you had to do?"

"What brought this on?" Dad asked.

"Got composition in class, tomorrow," he fibbed.

"We were in the trenches, mostly, except when Jerrie came at us or we went over the top for them."

"Well, what else?"

"Sometimes we went out on patrol."

He stopped looking out of the window and lifted some loose blank white sheets of paper and a pencil off the window ledge.

"Could you tell me about one of these, so I could write it down?"

He didn't immediately answer, as though he was giving the question some thought, was – perhaps – thinking about it or how he should react to the subject and what he thought to how he should answer the question? It was obviously important to his son, so he was careful not to respond flippantly.

"Not right now, your mum and I are slipping out to the top of the road for a quiet chat and a drink. You don't have to have it for tomorrow, d'you?"

He shook his head.

"No, I didn't think so," his dad concluded. "Tell you what, we'll talk about it over the weekend."

"Thanks, Dad."

"I'll…I'll think of something to give you to write down for that school composition, next time."

"Select any subject?" teacher told the class, answering a single query before they began to create their compositions. "It is the art," he told them, "of constructing sentences and of writing prose or verse. The practice or art of literary production," teacher further explained.

He thought about what his dad had told him and turned his words over in his mind before putting them to paper.

He called his article, The Sniper.

*His dad had recalled that one particular night, their company went over the top on patrol and before returning to their trenches. As the sniper, he'd been left out alone in 'no man's land'. Said it was very quiet in the darkness, but suddenly he heard movements. He immediately sought cover in a deserted and damaged farmhouse, nearby. He felt his way through the roofless house to steps that led down to a cellar, which he immediately scurried down into the darkness and crouched at what had been an air-vent at ground-level, on the dirt road outside. Very soon after, he heard a group of men come scrambling down the road toward the farmhouse. They halted close to the damaged dwelling and he heard them whispering to each other in German. Would they search the building, and worse, make their way into the cellar?*

*If they did and he was discovered…*

*He told his son that he was petrified with fear.*

*But then, almost instantly, there was the sound of a heavy exchange of machine-gun fire, not too distant away. He heard the sudden murmur and whispering as the men urgently and excitedly discussed the interruption. Then, to his profound relief, he heard them stealthily move off into the surrounding darkness.*

He used his dad's story as the framework and added more descriptive definition. He re-read his work, corrected spelling mistakes and re-wrote the composition, before submitting it for the tutor's perusal.

The Headmaster, pushing his spectacles high up onto the bridge of his prominent nose, stood before the senior class one early winter morning, and asked for a volunteer.

"We're fast approaching November and we all know what we used to celebrate, before the war, on the fifth of that month. – Anybody?"

This was the signal for much murmuring until one boy's hand shot up.

'Dixie', the Head, identified him. "Yes – go ahead?"

"Guy Fawkes night, sir."

"That's right. The gunpowder plot. – And what do we know about it? – Anybody?"

One boy said, in an almost inaudible voice. "Guy Fawkes tried to blow up the Houses of Parliament, sir."

"And why was that?" The Head immediately asked the class, making his way slowly down one of the aisles between the rows of occupied desks.

"Conspiracy, sir, by RCs to blow them up when the King visited on November the fifth, sir."

"Why?"

There was a hushed silence.

"Because," the Head informed, "they planned to kill the Protestant King and replace him, and so restore senior political Catholic leaders to former prominence. It's not quite all the truth, but it'll do for starters."

'Dixie' turned about and walked briskly back to the top of the class.

"Now," he said, turning to face the boys. "Who thinks he could write a play we could all act in to celebrate this event? Not about the reasons so much as the plotted action of conspiracy."

This invitation was greeted by stunned silence. This was not something they'd been urged to consider in the past, in any shape or form. It was pretty obvious, by the silence and lack of response, that there were no takers.

The Head's eyes roamed over the heads of the class as he walked back slowly down the aisle. He was making his mind up about something and he suddenly stopped at one desk and stared down with an unusual agreeable smile.

"How about you?" he probed, staring down hard through his specs.

The boy swallowed, unable to come up with a smart, but negative reply.

"That composition of yours about your father being a sniper in the Great War was very interesting. Showed promise?"

"Y-yes, sir," he managed.

"Yes, sir. So come to my office, after class, and we'll make a start."

He wanted to object, but the Head had already sped away and all he got were fleeting mischievous grins from some class mates, nearest where he sat all uncomfortable and in a slight state of shock.

Later, in the Head's study, he was beckoned to occupy a seat across and opposite him. The conversation worked its way along the lines that the Head wanted the class to involve and indulge itself in drama and stage study, which was what this exercise, he was told, was all about. The boy was to put together and write a short docudrama GUY FAWKES. It was to be a component part. The rest, would be those of his peers who would be likely attracted to the idea, and simultaneously in the hope that it would boost an interest for the rest becoming involved in the class project, which is what it was.

The class took to the idea like ducks-to-water, and with a week to go to 'bonfire night', were keen enough to work with each other in this one-act affair set in the pretend cellar beneath the pretend House of Lords.

The short production was performed and acted out on an afternoon during the last hour of the school day, in the main hall. There was a buzz of natural keenness amongst the boys. No costumes or stage furniture, but the scene was set by a narrator, reading from a script, to briefly describe the scene, before an assembly of combined school classes, gathered for this occasion.

The play went very well, with the characters holding their scripts in hand and reading from the hand-written texts on loose sheets of paper.

Although, practiced a few times beforehand and corrections sought and made, on the night – or afternoon, as it really was – there were a whole host of mistakes and miscues, which entertained the audience, no end. The 'actors' straining to get their parts right, and the audience no less enthused into noting the errors of continuity and enjoying the discovery with loud bursts of derisive laughter, much to the actors' embarrassments.

The Head's initial idea, again – although, barely accepted – was in finality a great treat, relaxing experiment and confining success, enjoyed by all involved and watching on.

## War News!

- Germans continue to fire a frightening new weapon against London, Britain's capital. V-1 flying bombs, 'Doodlebugs' or 'Buzz-Bombs' as they are called by the press, rain down on the undefended city. They are the product of intense research at Peenemunde, the German Army Research Centre, but operated and fired by the Luftwaffe from camouflaged bases in the Pas-de-Calais area of France.

## 13. Trouble A-Brewin

The boys were down on a piece of spare ground at the bottom of September Road, where it lay alongside a Liverpool Corporation yard, which was now producing Sherman tanks for the war. They were examining the shell of a gypsy caravan, parked there. It belonged to a family of Travellers who had been housed locally, and who's men folk it was said, had been inducted into the armed forces.

He stood, hands on his hips, and surveyed the outside of the vehicle, whilst some of his mates had clambered inside to examine it more closely.

All fittings were gone: either retrieved for safe keeping by the family until a later day or stolen. The windows, unfortunately, had all been bricked and were shattered and broken. A skylight in the ceiling was open to the elements and there was a good deal of damp penetration showing on wood walls and flooring. In fact, it was in a bit of a mess and would involve a lot of time, money and effort to put things right and to return it to its former state.

He considered the insides very cramped, and although the idea of travelling down some quiet country lane, drawn by a single horse or pony in harness, sounded ideal and could be considered highly idyllic, it didn't appeal to him.

'Uncle Mac' on BBC Children's Hour, Home Service, had a weekly programme during which a short sketch, with appropriate sound effects, was interesting enough to listen to, especially the wild life tips, but it still wasn't the sort of life he'd be attracted to.

However, he concluded, as he viewed the vandalism and resultant damage, it shouldn't have happened, but was somewhat placated by the knowledge that none of his mates were responsible for the mindless destruction.

His gaze drifted to the bomb-damaged house on Breckside Park Road, which backed out onto the edge of the Recreation Ground, behind it. It was the alleged location, where the boy out of his class, had accidentally fallen through damaged flooring and subsequently died of injuries sustained there.

He pondered on the recent worrying news that an event had occurred, which became a serious incident in his eyes and the thoughts of his mates. Of their concern, when they learned that a few friends of theirs, playing footie on the same area where inter-school football games were scheduled had been stopped and surrounded by a gang of 'no-marks' on the open ground.

The concern centred on the assumed authority by members of boy gangs whose homes were situated in the streets which were open to and led onto the Recreation Ground, and which they claimed – these nameless gangs – as being for their exclusive use and was therefore territorial domain or their pitch!

What actually happened, he heard from witnesses – local kids involved – was that a menacing group of these boys from

The Streets on the edge of the Recreation Ground, and which fed into Townsend Lane, took it onto themselves to 'police' the Recreation Ground, and that kids playing on it were subject to their adjudication. In effect, they – The Street's boys – would decide if those kids they challenged, be allowed to play there, based on where they were from in the surrounding area? Especially important was if the boys from The Streets had previously planned a game there, and discovered strangers in situ on their stomping ground, so-to-speak, a dispute would arise as to who had the right of play?

The lads from September, August, July and Gloucester Roads always believed that the Recreation Ground was free for anyone.

Nobody had any right to preside over anybody else.

The space was on a first-come-first-served basis.

The Streets gang made sure, by force of numbers, that they had the final say!

This was something new and worrying to the kids off Lower Breck Road, and not something to be taken lightly. In fact, when some of them met together, after hearing about at least two incidents which had occurred very recently, it was decided that they must have a big pow-wow and reach a decision – and quickly – as to what they should do and how to go about it?

## War News!

- Battle of the Falaise Gap drawing to a close as Allied troops seal off escape routes for German 7th and Panzer 5th Army remnants trapped there.
- Warsaw uprising has become a bloody confrontation between ill-equipped resistance fighters and well-armed German troops. Uprising was only planned to last for several days to enable and give Russian forces chance to enter the city and relieve them. Soviets, puzzlingly, halted their advance on the city?

# 14. Higgie and PT

It was while he was working on his class work, that he heard the class room door open and shut. No interest in that, but a shadow subsequently passed across his desk as a class mate clumsily pushed past. Glancing up, he saw Higgie's back, edging across to where his empty desk awaited him. There was nothing special or out of the ordinary about that, except that there was a nagging unanswered question that jumped to mind, with H's appearance.

Since the incident which occurred a week ago, when inexpressibly H had stoned a greengrocer's shop window on Lower Breck Road, he'd been absent from school due to illness, it was said. He'd also heard that H's mother had moved home into the West Derby district, due to some domestic problem or other?

Whatever?

The fact remained, that the incident had involved him in a very nasty and unpleasant, embarrassing situation. H, as he recalled painfully, disappeared so quickly after hurling the stone at the window of the shop, that those shocked customers and staff inside who instantly whirled to see who'd thrown the stone, saw only a single boy. They all decided that the boy who stared back at the smashed window with shocked countenance, was the stone thrower.

He'd abruptly vacated the scene.

Even now, he still cringed as the mental images retuned to haunt him.

All those shocked grown-ups staring through the shattered remains of the window directly at him!

They'd all be willing to witness he was the 'erk' who'd lobbed the stone at the window. They'd be believed, because they were all adults and nobody would believe a snivelling lying little nobody of a snotty-nosed kid.

Over the next week, he avoided, like a plague, going anywhere near Lower Breck Road in his travels.

During the mid-morning break, he hunted H down and found him puffing on a Woodbine ciggie behind the brick-built urinals, and talking confidentially to his cousin, Richie, whom he knew, because he lived further up September Road, from him.

His approach didn't go unnoticed by H and he broke off conversation to turn his way. H grinned, as though he could read the question in his mind.

"Been to the shops on Lower Breck Road, lately?" he teased, smirking conspiratorially.

Shaking his head and half smiling, but not really amused, said. "I don't get it?"

"What? – Get what?" H's voice responded, a note higher, with a smirk still idling around his mouth.

"Stoning that shop?"

H turned and glanced at Richie and sniggered. "Your mate got himself in a spot of bother," he confided.

"NO! Not me," he responded.

H continued to Richie. "Police sergeant came to the school, in the afternoon, an' you shudda seen his face! I pointed out the scuffer's helmet showing in the Head's study, through the winder."

"Higgie…"

"An' he – " He giggled, pointing at him as Richie watched on – "wet himself!"

"Wasn't like that!"

"You thought…"

"You were sick, because you wus sure the Scuffer had come straight from the shop," H positively screeched in laughter, hardly able to continue.

Due to H's infectious laughter, Richie was smitten and began to grin.

He didn't get to ask H why he'd thrown the stone and at that shop, in particular?

It bothered him some, because he had – or thought he had? – the instinctive ability to suss out what other kids were thinking, but in H's case, he realised this was not so? Why H had done this was a shocker and out of the blue. He didn't see it coming and this was what shook him: not having the pre-notion of H's wilful act? He considered H to be an odd ball because nothing seemed to bother him. Like H had a strong conviction in himself: an unshakeable belief in himself and didn't give a hoot for what others might think or say about him.

"You gonna fight, this after?" H grinned, changing the subject.

Perplexed, he said, "Fight?"

"Dixie told us yester afternoon, the top class would be having boxing as a PT workout today, for the last hour."

"News to me!" he replied, lightly, in disbelief.

"You no likee?" H challenged.

"Where?"

"Said we could push the desks aside. Said he'd got some kids boxing gloves we can wear."

"Who's boxing who?"

H screwed up his face in thought. "Dunno?"

"Not everybody will want to?"

"Well, Dixie said on'y those that want to?"

He didn't comment.

"Does that include you?" H continued, eyebrows raised, jeeringly.

He didn't reply, because at that moment the bell calling the boys back to class, interrupted their conversation.

He wasn't given the chance or the opportunity to bring it up again – the stone through the shop window, and knew he might never know why?

There was a good deal of excitement that afternoon, when the top class in the last hour of the school day, helped move desks-n'-chairs to the sides of the room to create space for the boxing workout.

Dixie, the Head, was liked by almost all the boys. 'Course, there was always one or two odd-balls who didn't like him, maybe feared him for one reason or another? Then, they probably didn't like any teacher or disciplines that went with traditional education. In fact, they probably didn't even like themselves?

Dixie was all go. Had to be, the class reckoned, when his name arose, because there was a teacher shortage due to the war, which meant he was called upon to be here, there and everywhere, during the school day. Didn't have time for hiccups in the form of difficult pupils and did use the cane to maintain order. However, the class agreed amongst themselves that he was 'fair' and that some of the activities one or two got up to, deserved all they got, in the form and liberal use of the cane.

Dixie, it was, who had the class out in the yard on a cold, but dry, winters' mornings for PT, before commencing their lessons. Told them, it would wake them up and prepare them for the day!

The four pairs of boxing gloves of different sizes, well used and worn, were produced. Already, those prepared 'to have a go' had assembled in one corner of the room with much good humour, laughter and noisy commotion.

The Head, who was also to be the referee, told them that the matches would be two two-minute affairs or less if it became too one-sided. The boys were all about the same age, but this parity ended there, because they were a mix of tall-n'-short, fat-n'-skinny. However, the approach, by the whole class, was all good natured enough.

He stood alongside Higgie, who was matched with Brooksie, a tall, but recognised bully-boy. When they gloved-up and moved to the centre of the open space, joining Dixie in the middle, the height disparity was clearly evident. B towering head-n'-shoulders over H, who was kind of short, but chunky of build. Also, H was an unknown character, unpredictable and inconsistent.

First bout, introduced by Dixie in the manner of a boxing radio commentator, was greeted with much amusement in the room. The boys in normal dress, minus jackets or blazers, but in jersey and shirts, some with rolled-up cuffs.

Dixie shook a hand bell in his hand and the first two boys ran at each other and ended up wrestling, rather than boxing, except for clinching; then both fell to the floor together, to the joyful glee of the shouting noisy audience of watchers. One boy stayed down, however, and waved an arm of surrender, but laughing as he did so, and was helped to his feet by his opponent. It was that sort of affair. Not seriously considered but gone into with amused anticipation: a general knockabout.

The second bout was no different in endeavour than the first one, 'cepting that one of the boys was obese and used his weight behind a goat-like head to butt into his opponent's midriff – oops, solar plexus, accompanied by a roar of dismissive boos! After he'd tried this on two more times, Dixie brought the clash to an end and disqualified him, much to the delight of all assembled and to cheers of agreement. Obese seemed to agree also, because his blood red shining cheeks, beamed openly.

Came the Higgie versus Brooksie scrap, and it was a much more serious affair. H started off in intense mood and deftly danced around and out of range from the wild mad rushes B attempted; then suddenly H sprang into action and launched himself two-fisted at the taller boy in front of him. It was clear to see that H had the skills as a scrapper, because he paused after one step-aside and flung a flurry of punches, coming back again, counter-punching and catching B open-mouthed and floundering – off-balance. H followed him, as B stepped awkwardly and clumsily away to try to avoid the thumping boxing gloves which were finding their mark on his face and sides of his unprotected head. Here was a boy very handy with his dukes, there was no doubt about that. The crowd of kids watching, fell back in a swaying wave to give the two battlers room to move. B was clearly unhappy. B then threw himself forward, H stood his ground and hurled a ferocious volley of punches.

Brooksie was down!

-Had his head tucked as best he could between his raised knees.

Dixie was across the room and grabbing hold of a victorious H to the loud cheers and popular acclaim for winner in the last bout of the day, but despite the cheers from his class mates, H remained po-faced and showed no emotion.

### War News!

- The city of Riga in Latvia is stormed by Soviet troops of their northern command wing and cleared of German forces.
- Government urges army to do something about the V-1 terror bombing. Army arranges for massing of anti-aircraft batteries on the eastern approaches to the capital, in an effort to confront and control the effectiveness of these attacks.

# 15. Battle of Breckside Park

Kids' problems are sometimes connected to free access and right of way – their right of way. The chat amongst the kids from September Road and other nearby roads and side streets, was of concern. It centred on the Recreation Ground, or as they commonly referred to it as 'Breckside Park', which was not really a true description, but everyone – locally – knew where and what they were talking about.

Generally, the discussion followed the course of wait-n'-see. In other words, do nothing and it would go away. Seemed like, that was the right decision after about ten days or so – wrong!

Two weeks after that assumption, it was said that the 'Streets Gang' had chased four local kids – September/Gloucester Roads – off the park, who'd been playing a game of footie.

He, and a couple of others from his road, took a run over there to the Recce Ground, to have a look-see at what was going on?

There were, as far as they could see in the distance, some of the Streets Gang perched up and squatting on some extended Anderson shelters, which had been constructed for the residents at the end of the Streets, and some hundred feet or so into the grounds of Breckside Park. The minute they showed, arriving and emerging from the Entry between the Liverpool Corporation yard and the bomb-damaged house, they were immediately spotted. Members of the gang could be seen pointing in their direction with all faces turned their way and watching. Seconds later, they all stood: a straggle line of about seven or eight of them, aged something-like between nine and twelve, with hands on their hips. It was a provocative stance. They were waiting to see what the 'intruders' intended.

The September three, observed the scene briefly, before turning and retracing their steps back through the Entry. In the face of obvious provocation, there was nothing else they wanted to do, but withdraw and think it over, which they did.

Clearly, the Streets Gang had decided to deny anybody they didn't accept from playing there – or even crossing over it with other destinations in mind. For the three-some, to have wandered aimlessly onto the Grounds, would have ensured a confrontation or even an attack on them. The outcome, no matter how brave they thought they were, would have been the height of folly and foolishness.

A day or more passed. More informal chat between kids from the Lower Breck Road neighbourhood took place. It was agreed that a decision had to be made to, (a) avoid that area for playing footie, or (b) they went elsewhere? The eventual outcome of their verbals with each other was that the Streets Gang should be taught a lesson and one that they'd not forget.

He recalled the Streets Gang squatting on the extended air-raid shelters and his mind immediately turned to counting heads, and the numbers game came to the fore. His road, he figured, could probably muster about nine boys around his age of twelve-ish going on thirteen, and that included all the boys who played footie together, or were classmates at the local school, with one or two thrown in who weren't attendees at his school, but lived in the road. Then there were other kids they kind of knew to wave or chat with who lived in adjacent roads, like August, July and Gloucester.

How to get the word out for a pow-wow?

Easy enough. Kid's 'bush telegraph' through chatter in school, and 'pass the word': old bomb-damaged house by the Corpy yard, after school.

At first, just a sprinkling of kids he knew and mixed with – mostly from the road. More trickled in, like five curious listening frowns from August and three from July Roads. Amongst these making an appearance, was Brooksie and his bessy mate.

He viewed B's inclusion with dark suspicion. He wasn't strictly from their area, and certainly hadn't been invited. B and his friend, he noticed, stood off to one side at the back of the group, to listen. Always seemed to have a scowl on his face. B would be up to no good, he was sure, but for the time being the meeting and plans to work out their problem, was more important.

Didn't take long, as he called the boys together, from a knot of high ground in the back garden of the deserted, bomb-damaged, deserted and window-less old house. He called to two of the boys, who'd been harassed and chased by the Streets Gang to come up beside him and tell what happened, which they were only too eager to tell. There then followed a loose exchange of chat about how they felt about this threat, what should be done, and a plan of action?

Wasn't too hard for them to finally arrive and a united and determined decision to call a halt to the menacing challenge. All agreed with shouts and fists raised and shaken in the air above their heads, that a deterrent was needed, no warning to be given, and that the only answer was the big stick! More cheers and shouted oaths from a sea of excited eyes in shiny faces showed the feeling of the boys. Thoughts then quickly moved on to organisation and planning.

"What about the cinder path?" shouted one.

He understood the question and in his mind's eye had a picture of the path in question which ran from one corner by the Entry to the Corpy yard diagonally across the grounds to the swing corner at the top end which almost led to the Cabbage Hall Picture House.

"What about it?" he asked.

"Grown-ups use it."

"So we'll wait until the path is empty," and then added, "we'll wait until tomorrow – Saturday, when there shouldn't be many adults using the path. To start with, we must find out how far we can hurl stones from behind this wall?" he said, patting the chipped, mortar-cracked and broken brickwork of the rear garden wall, that backed onto the recreation ground. He also pointed at the wide break in the wall, around the middle section, which was about four feet wide by six foot high.

Perplexed and puzzled faces stared back.

"Want two boys to go out through the hole, there, and onto the Grounds, but stand well apart," he instructed, and added, "Have you got your markers?"

Each boy flourished a feathered duster on short bamboo, they'd managed to lift from their mother's broom-closets.

"You six on the first row, collect stones lying around and form a line behind the wall," which they rushed to do, enjoying what they considered to be a great game.

"Okay, when I count Three, throw the stones as far over the wall onto the Recce Ground as far as you can toward where you think the markers might be. One, Two – Three!"

Half-a-dozen small stones which fitted comfortably into the boy's hands, went whizzing over the wall and onto the deserted and empty Grounds.

"You two, out there, stick those markers where you saw the stones land, or you think the stones landed," he shouted, then turning to the throwers, told them, "those dusters are markers for when we lure the Streets Gang to chase our three fastest runners, who'll tempt them into a chase."

"Oh YEAH!" shouted one, getting the picture and rising to the occasion.

"Get your stone store together, so that when they get within the range of our markers, we throw everything we've got. They should be straddled; then we pour out through the hole in the wall sticks-n'-brush handles and chase after them. Any we catch, we give their legs an' arses a battering…"

"Y-E-S-s-s-s…" the boys chorused in response, looking forward to the action more and more.

"What about us havin' a flag?" one bright spark, squeaked.

He hadn't thought about that, but when the boy's idea was seconded by others, he changed his mind.

"Okay, leave that to me, yeah?"

The meeting, however, was temporarily interrupted by the arrival of three twelve-year-old girls. He stopped speaking and stared out from the top of the mound over the tousled heads of the boys in front of him at the girl's arrival. One, he immediately recognised, as the sister to one of the lads in front of him, and the other two he reasoned must've been her friends she'd dragged along.

The brother of the girl had turned and noticed their presence and told her in a gruff voice and with a frown. "This is a boy's meeting. Not for yous gerls, 'kay?"

Stood on higher ground, he could see they were immediately peeved and didn't take kindly to the brother's advice, until an idea occurred to him.

"You can come as nurses, if you want?" he shouted his inspired invitation.

He could see the boys were not so sure.

The girls, meanwhile, put their heads together and instantly turned smiley faces in agreement with nodding heads of long loose hair.

"Go home and get some white hankies and germoline ointment, but don't let anybody see you taking them, and – defo – don't tell anybody what you want it for, if they asks!"

"When d'you want us back?" Sis shrilled, the three now excited by their inclusion.

"Sat'day morning…ten o'clock."

Still, all smiles, they nodded and sped away.

He rose early, Saturday morning, foregoing his lie-in. Reason for his early rise was the promise to supply a flag. Easier said than done! Immediately to mind was to find and use the union flag, commonly known as the 'Union Jack'. He didn't have one, and he needed one for ten o'clock. Managed to get an old piece of old marked-up white bed sheet off his mum, who was so busy cleaning the bedrooms and making the beds, she didn't ask him what it was for? He cut it with a pair of scissors into a two-foot by two-foot square shape.

What emblem could he try to fit or paint onto it? He knew it would have to be something simple and easy to do, because he was no artist. With his box of water-paints on the edge of the table and the white sheet open flat and laid on last night's Echo newspaper, it was ready for his master-piece?

Like magic, an idea came to mind, having seen the emblem in a photograph in the newspaper that week. At the time it had caught his eye, but now it became an important symbol and one he could emulate. He copied out the symbol from memory. Marked out – smeared, would have been a better description – the Free French symbol 'Cross of Lorraine'. When he'd finished his handy-work, he found a bamboo cane, and with two short pieces of string, two holes punched through the material, he secured it to the top half of the bamboo. He flourished it above his head and was satisfied with the effort, before folding it carefully and putting it to one side to take with him when he went to meet up with the boys at the rendezvous at ten-ish, that morning.

He checked the weather and was pleased to note that although the sky was overcast, it wasn't raining. This could've scuppered the whole plan, because the Streets Gang wouldn't turn out in the rain and probably wouldn't be interested in whoever wandered across Breckside Park. Most kids, he reasoned, don't like getting wet in rain showers, no matter what the interest outside the house.

Most of the boys had assembled, working and running around searching for and collecting small stones to build heaped piles of them at intervals behind the wall, but within the overgrown, derelict and abandoned garden.

He edged up to the opening in the wall to stare out and try to identify movement on the other side of the Recreation Ground.

Nothing stirred.

He returned to mix and talk with the lads, and as he did so, others arrived to swell the ranks. The girls had turned up, also. They wore men's large white handkerchiefs tied-on head coverings, concealing their hair, with a red cross marked brightly with the use of somebody's lipstick, on the top. They also carried little cloth bags with a multitude of first-aid contents, including, cotton wool swobs, wound dressings, sealing tape, scissors, safety pins, bottle of iodine, a half full brown bottle of cough mixture with a small silver apostle tea spoon, after raiding their home medical boxes or containers, telling the boys when they asked, that they were ready and equipped to administer instant dubious medical assistance! Some of the boys were not convinced.

Within the short span of the next fifteen minutes, the boys mustered sixteen junior warriors, 'cepting the nursing auxiliaries.

The group cheered when he unveiled their colours with a side-to-side flashy flourish of their newly commissioned flag: a red Cross-of-Lorraine. Some were puzzled by the emblem, but he shrugged off any complaint. It was all part of the game. They hadn't had this much fun to look forward to in a long time. Uppermost in their thinking was the coming event and were carried away with heady excitement and anticipation.

He knew they didn't consider him as their 'leader', because just about any of them could've taken charge of what they were about to do and the plan sounded right.

Now, they were ready!

He beckoned forward the three self-proclaimed fastest runners and led them to the opening. First off, he glanced across 'no man's land'. In the distance, he picked out two or three young seven-year-olds playing tick on the extended shelters.

He waved the runners forward with the advice that they were not to get too close to 'enemy territory' and when the Streets Gang mustered and began running at them to cut them off or encircle them, they were to show a clean pair of heels and head for home, pronto!

That he'd be watching over the wall to give the signal to the other kids to be prepared.

Three serious heads nodded in unison, and scrambled out through the hole in the wall, heading to cross the cinder path and to approach the Anderson shelters.

He jumped back, after they'd left, and attended to selecting a standard-bearer and to inspect the stone piles. After which, he inspected the rest of the troops, and noticed two of the boys sporting ARP 'steel helmets with a large 'W' painted on the front, and the remains of several month's conglomeration of dust and remains of cobwebs. Another wore motor-cycle goggles, that needed a good clean. Their weapons, included two thin 3-foot-long branches pulled off a tree, a damaged yard-brush with half a head, black bicycle pump, an old man's walking stick, torn gent's umbrella, split cricket bat, laundry-line wooden prop and a catapult. Three of the boys also carried dust-bin lids as shields, slid over their left wrists onto their forearms.

They were all geared up and excited because they knew the time of confrontation was near, and they'd have the chance to prove their bravery to each other!

He was slightly concerned. What he considered, earlier, was not a problem or threat to the plan, was – in fact – in danger of becoming one. From his position at the wall, he'd followed with his eyes the furtive advance of his three decoys, but noticed also, the figures of two middle-aged women on the cinder path in charge of a little black-n'-white pet mongrel dog, off the lead and scurrying here, there and everywhere, inspecting clumps of grass and…his markers! They old ladies were talking animatedly and loudly together and seemed in no hurry, as they dawdled along.

He bit his lip in vexation and tried to 'will' them to move at a faster pace, in vain, of course.

The decoys had split up and fanned out, ten feet apart, but continued to advance toward the shelters, but only when they thought the kids playing tick, had not noticed their movements, otherwise, they'd halt and crouch down low. They wanted and needed to get as close and as near as possible, before they were noticed, to give themselves more time in the final stage of luring the Street Gang into a general chase and pursuit, – and to avoid any pincer trap the Gang might try to spring.

From his position at the top of the wall, it didn't look like this was going to happen, that way. For starters, the women's pet dog was a little yap-yap, and proved it after discovering, sniffing out and being surprised by one of the crouching figures in the grass. It kicked-off in a barking frenzy in front of one of the decoys.

This noise halted the women's conversation, whilst they stared off in the direction and cause of the disturbance, as their little pet doggie-wog confronted something they couldn't see, in the long grass.

It also attracted and alerted the curiosity of the seven-year-olds playing together in the area of the extended shelters.

He watched as the kids ran together and chatter like a troop of monkeys, standing up tall and pointing toward where the decoys were crouching, trying to assess how many there were and their direction of advance? Kids are as bright as a penny when it comes to picking up danger signs. Got quick good eye-sight, too. They suddenly peeled off and ran pel-mel back to the Streets.

He realised this was as close as the decoys were going to get. The woman's little pet, still continued to flag-up its discovery with more loud, squeaky bursts of hysterical barking.

The decoys stood up from their concealment, looked at each other and then back to the hole-in-the-wall, for further guidance.

"Them women an' their dog are a bloody nuisance," one of the boys swore, stood by his side and peering through the opening in the top of the wall, at what was taking place before them.

"Tell me about it?" he said, disappointed at how this part of his plan was shaping up.

He waved to the decoys to crouch down again and await signs of movement beyond the shelters, in and around the Streets. They were unsure of his meaning, so he pointed to his eyes and then over their heads. The hand signals seemed to satisfy them and the three crouched down, waiting and watching ahead.

Over the next five to ten minutes, there was no sign of activity from the shelters area, but the two ladies had finally, and with difficulty, managed to recall and grab their darling little bow-wow, and had reversed their walk and ambled off – presumably – back home, disappearing from the cinder track, which was now deserted and ideal for the plan.

Possibly, he'd overlooked some places near the shelter area, because out of the corner of his eyes, he saw heads bobbing up and down behind them at the extreme opposite ends of where the shelters had been built.

The 'enemy' were attempting to outflank and trap the decoys.

He stood up in the hole-in-the-wall and beckoned to the three runners to return, pronto! Which they did, because they'd sighted the significant threat at about the same time as he had.

They stood, wheeled and bolted back, as a horde of screaming, yelling young bodies emerged and launched themselves from both ends of the shelter line, in an avenging mob.

Clearly, the decoys had a good lead and came bounding to the 'bolt-hole' in the garden wall, at full gallop. The three arrived, breathing hard, half hysterical with excited laughter and thoroughly enjoying themselves.

He patted them in as they squeezed past him onto the overgrown garden of the bomb-damaged house and as they did so, they became aware of their comrades already stood and positioned next to their own particular stone piles, individual stones already gripped in the palms of their hands, ready and poised to begin hurling missiles, when the signal was given.

At his post alongside the opening in the wall, he watched the ragged approach of the Streets Gang mob, whooping, bawling and howling.

He watched more keenly as their front runners bore down on the feather-duster markers, poking up out of the ground.

He took in the fact that their forward runners had outraced the general body of pursuers, and so took into account the need to delay his signal until the main body of the mob crossed the invisible line.

He figured there was about seven or eight of them, with younger kids running catch-up.

"NOW!" he shouted, twisting to ensure the stone-throwers had got the message.

First volley soared into the air and over the wall, climbing and then plummeting down and onto the heads-n'-shoulders of the main body of the Streets Gang.

Immediately, there were shouts of alarm and even a lone cry, as the missiles struck unprotected, heads, shoulders, arms and legs.

He saw the horde pause in their charge and then stop, colliding with each other as they did so, in a confused and a further disordered rabble.

The boys in the garden had already reached, selected and launched a second volley of stones, which straddled the scrambling shambles, still trying to make sense of what was happening to them.

He saw the bewilderment registered in their eyes and faces, which decided him on triggering their counter-attack.

"LET'S GET 'EM!" he roared.

The garden boys, yelling loudly, scrabbled to collect their weapons and ran straight at the opening, jostling to squeeze through, spilling out onto the Recce Ground, much to the amazement and distress of the Streets Gang, who instantly – almost as one – turned turtle and fled back toward the extended Anderson shelters, following and swiftly pursued by a cheering mob of September and other adjoining Road boys from the opening, flag-bearer in the vanguard, all very organised and prepared to catch and give them a thrashing.

The Streets Gang had been completely surprised and routed by events.

They were unprepared for this counter-aggression.

He was with and alongside the flag-bearer as they caught up with the stragglers from the Streets Gang, who were already being swiped on the legs and buttocks.

Suddenly, out of nowhere, two workmen in overalls turned the corner from the Entry onto the cinder path, having left the Corpy yard.

They saw what was happening and rushed into the centre of the fight to break it up, which they did. Trapped Streets Gang members saw their chance, scampered away and escaped. The boys from the garden opening, abruptly stopped, backed off and headed reluctantly toward the bomb-damaged house.

They all did, in the face of this unexpected interference by the workmen.

They didn't fight grown-ups!

**War News!**

- British Forces occupy Greek capital Athens. Restore order as Left – wing units try to take over in the vacuum left by retreating German garrison.

## 16. Reds 'n' Blues

"Are you a Toffee?" one of the two boys on the wall asked him.

"Well, I am and I'm not," he replied vaguely.

"What kinda answer is that?" said the other.

"My dad goes, when he can."

"To Goodison Park?" the first boy queried.

The other interrupted with a cynical comment, "Well, it wouldn't be Anfield, would it?"

"How do I know?" the first boy defended. "I asked him if he was a Toffee, not his dad."

"Gladys Street," he confirmed to both of them.

"And you?" the first boy continued. "D'you go with 'im?"

"'Course, when he goes, but there's a war on, so it isn't like before the war, with the First Division."

"Football League Northern Section," the boy supplied, grinning, and added as an afterthought. "Nowadays."

"That's right."

"But what d'you mean, 'I am, an' I'm not'?"

He licked his lips, and then said. "When Everton's playing at Goodison Park."

"And?"

"When Liverpool are at home, I go – with the – er, lads from school."

"So, why is that?" the inquisitive boy persisted.

He didn't answer, immediately.

"Okay, why?" the boy pressed him.

He struggled with an answer because he didn't really want to continue with the subject.

His accuser followed on from his own question. "Everton's First Division Team. Liverpool…well, they're down in the Second Division, or they was, before the war. When the war's over and the regular football start up again, they'll STILL be on in the Second Division."

"I know that," he said quickly.

"Does…does yer dad know?"

"Know what?"

"That…you're Blues one week, an' a turncoat the next?"

"It's not like that," he protested, slightly peeved.

"So," the boy, swung around arms outstretched and giving his other mate a signal and knowing glance. "What's it like?"

"Ey!" he reacted, sternly. "There's other kids in this road that go to Anfield, too."

"And," the boy stepped forward and closer to him. "We all know who they are, but yous run with the hares an' hunt with the hounds, eh?"

"If you must know," he reacted, resentfully. "Goodison is always packed and overcrowded most of the time. I can't follow the game, because the crowd is always swaying backwards and forwards, and when I go with my pals from school to Anfield, there's always plenty of room."

"Where, in Anfield?"

"In the Kop."

"That rusty cow shed, with all the holes letting the rain through?"

He shook his head and half laughed sarcastically, in response.

"So," his interrogator asked, "were yous there, the week of the 'Derby game'?"

"Nil Nil, wasn't it?"

"You tell me. Youse was there?"

"Didn't go."

"Anyways, last week we flattened your lot, two-nil at Goodison."

"Yeah, I know. I was there."

"With yer dad?"

"Right."

"Reds 'as got NO chance against us Tricky Blue Boys," the boy goaded triumphantly, and continuing. "So, are yous right at the back in the Kop or at the front?"

"Middle."

"An' yous can see from there?"

"We sit on the bar."

This time it was the boy's turn to stay silent.

He smiled in the face of silence. "Got a shock the first time I went," he ventured.

"Shock?"

"Me school mates sit on the bar and moved along so-as I could climb up there and sit beside them. They made a space for me, so I climbed on up and clamped both hands either side of my bottom on the bar. Hadn't been, but a minute or so, when the ball got kicked up field toward the Kop end and skimmed the cross bar of the goal. Fellahs behind me, swayed forward and one bloke pressed his hand between my shoulder-blades to steady himself. Next thing I knew, I was hangin' upside down, underneath the bar, holdin' on for dear life!" he chuckled, remembering the episode.

"Upside down?" they chortled.

He giggled some more. "Like a bat," and his own laughter at himself, stopped him adding further comment.

### War News!

- General Douglas MacArthur authorises the amphibious invasion of the Gulf of Leyte in the Philippines, which had been occupied by the Japanese since 1942. Shortly after, naval action between units of US surface vessels and Japanese Imperial Naval units, takes place in and around the vicinity. The outcome of this action was considered to be an outstanding victory at sea, in favour of the United States Pacific Fleet.

# 17. An Unexpected Interruption at the Picture House

The Lido Picture House on Belmont Road was not considered by the September Road boys to be a particularly luxurious cinema, compared to other local flea pits.

In fact, it was seldom a Picture-Palace that he looked for in the columns advertising films showing at local cinemas on the front page of the Liverpool Echo. Mostly, they were dated British flicks and old American reel exports.

Interest was sparked by him and his pals, when they showed some Old Mother Riley films, made by British National Films, starring Arthur Lucan and Kitty McShane, like 'OLD MOTHER RILEY JOINS UP!' the storyline of which takes place during WWII. Always uproarious escapades. In this particular film, Mother Riley is a nurse who volunteers for the Auxiliary Territorial Services during which she detects and reports a nest of Nazi spies who are trying to steal secret government documents.

Always good for a laugh, but they agreed the best one they'd seen and which gave them hours of jocular and hilarious recalled amusement, was the film 'OLD MOTHER RILEY'S GHOST', when she inherits a haunted Scottish castle and disrupts an espionage ring who are trying to steal an inventor's plans.

The Lido Cinema used to be good for the Charlie Chan films, starring Sydney Toler. All American west coast mysteries of crime and spymaster intrigue occurring during the early years of WWII, but a good ninety minutes of weird and unorthodox sleuthing. Especially films like 'Charlie Chan in 'THE SECRET SERVICE' and produced by Monogram Pictures. His energetic chauffer was Number Three Son, played by Benson Fong ably assisted by Number Two Daughter Iris, Marianne Quon. In this instance, the plot line showed Charlie Chan as a US government agent out to find the killer of a torpedo inventor, and as the picture progresses, proves successful.

Sometimes, they had come away from one of these 'House's-of-Dreams' with the feeling they'd been robbed, because he and his mates had found the main feature was a crashing bore, even though they always watched everything, including Pathe News, coming attractions for the following Sunday; then Monday, Tuesday and Wednesday features, followed by what was on, come Thursday, Friday and Saturday. 'Course, there might be a short film from the Ministry of Food? Whatever, they'd sit through everything, getting their money's worth, up to and until the reels came around to when they'd first sat down, the performances being continuous.

Excitement wasn't confined solely to the flashing screen…

He'd remembered one particular time when sat with two pals, lounging back in the seat and watching a tedious and monotonous love scene. The young couple ahead of them and in the row in front, were fidgety and fussing with each other between giggles. Then, the young man in the row in front, offered his 'sweetheart' a cigarette, which she refused.

This was when the fun – really started.

He stuck the cigarette between his own lips, Humphrey Bogart style, pulled out a cigarette lighter from his jacket pocket, fumbled with it, thumbed the striker wheel to flash up the wick and so light his cigarette.

*Click!*

*WHOOF!*

A blue-red explosion of flame flashed eight inches up from the lighter, which he instinctively released from his burning fingers to let drop and bounce off his knees, which had straightened as he jack-knifed to his feet, the still flaming lighter then bouncing down onto the floor and sliding forward under the seat of the unfortunate patron in front, which was occupied by a very plump lady wearing a tiny hat with a tall feather, protruding.

Immediately, the heat-n'-light of the burning lighter took the form of a 'Molotov cocktail'!

The woman became electrified as one brief startled glance down between her knees, caught sight of the inferno.

Then, and with a terrifying shriek that alerted the whole picture house, she leapt to her feet, her seat sent crashing back loudly against the seat frame.

"AGH-H-h-h-h!"

Pandemonium raged for perilous mini-seconds.

Heads in all the rows, swivelling to stare wide-eyed and open mouthed toward the centre of their concern.

Made suddenly worse, moments later, when a slip-of-a-girl in cinema usherette's uniform, appeared instantly at the end of the row, swaying uncertainly, under the weight of a fire extinguisher cylinder clasped tightly to her tiny bosom, and could be plainly seen trying, hurriedly frowning, to speed-read the instructions printed in black on the red metal canister for the first time in her life! – Whilst her left hand grappled and struggled, scratching to pull the hose free and point it uncertainly and dangerously along a full row of seated and suddenly very alarmed patrons, instantly aware that there was worse to come, even as – already – some of the highly nervous and agitated audience had instinctively hidden behind a collection of hoped-for protective folded raincoats, handbags, caps and trilbies to ward off the shock of the expected deluge of white foam certain to splash across and against them…

Incredibly, the instant source of heat-n-flames, extinguished itself, mysteriously…

In a flash, sanity was restored.

The hazard resolved!

Miraculously, and a great deal faster than the 7$^{th}$ Cavalry, the towering and portly figure of the Picture House uniformed doorman-come-fireman, magically appeared at the usherette's side and snatched away the canister out of her uncertain nervous hands in the nick of time.

The 'Oh, No!' was frozen on the lips of a jumbled half-seated and shocked cinemagoers.

Threat was past…

Peace was restored.

Immediately, great sighs, fits of excitable coughing and the loud hum of emotional verbal uttered relief, the individuals on the row reacting in their own way: trembling awkward body movement, shuffling, quick short pealing cackle of muffled laughter, collecting their wits, their composure – what was left of it, and reasserting their self-esteem with smiling faces to hide a possible sense of certain derisory personal exposure and subsequent humiliation.

**War News!**

- British 8th Army drive north along the Italian Adriatic coast, broke the German Gothic Line at Pesaro; then surged on to capture Rimini, and together with the US 5th Army reached a position just south of Bologna.
- Last defensive position in Belgium occupied by German troops at Zeebrugge, is attacked and captured by elements of the Canadian 3rd Infantry Division as part of Operation Switchback.
- RAF Lancasters 4-engined heavy bombers attack and sink German battleship Tirpitz with 12,000lb 'Tallboy' bombs as she was at anchor near Tromso, Norway.

# 18. Fourth Estate

He was sat at his desk during English composition, staring idly out through the classroom window at the rush of dark-grey rain clouds propelled by a nor-westerly wind.

Whilst he enjoyed the relaxation, having completed and finished his class essay, the thought crossed his mind that it would be exciting to be the editor of a newspaper, writing, reflecting and reaching opinions on world events, especially how the Allies were advancing on all fronts against a common enemy with an agreed end in sight.

But how?

That part of it his idea slowed and halted his thoughts.

How?

The teacher's voice broke into his conception, instructing the class to make sure their name was printed at the top right of the sheet, before passing them forward for collection and subsequent marking.

Out in the yard, during mid-morning break, he was preoccupied again by his previous speculation on the subject. What were those jobs, again? Reporter, journalist, feature writer, editor…In his mind, the titles of that profession sounded like the sort of work involvement that attracted him.

Hadn't young Winston been a scribe for one of the London broadsheets, during his stint in the Boar War? That job title earned him the right to be allowed to travel along with troop moments supplying the men, together with supplies to the garrison towns, to become part of the defensive perimeter, and to ride out with the reconnaissance units to seek out and observe enemy movements on the ground; then to write and file his reports back to London for the editor of the newspaper.

The very thought of it stimulated his imagination.

It didn't take much to do that either he mentally allowed.

The scenarios were as good and as exciting as a western backdrop out in Texas or Colorado, or…But then, he realised, how difficult it would be to attain that sort of accomplishment.

Back to Square One, as a snotty-nosed scouser attending Elementary School, aged just twelve years. Didn't look or seem likely that this would happen or materialise, any time soon? Besides, he reasoned sadly, this sort of opportunity didn't avail itself to the likes of a nobody like him! Needed the training that went with a Grammar School education, followed by years of intense study at university.

The bell sounded and he was soon back in class, sat at his desk with his shared maths book open, between other pupils alongside and peering over his shoulder, due to the shortage of books to go around. There was a war on, he'd been informed, when he'd raised the subject at an earlier date.

After school and at home, his previous concentration returned to stir up and renew his curiosity. He dragged on his thinking cap, while stroking his pet cat, tail high and pressing it's puny silky-haired body against his legs, gently purring.

He didn't have a printing press but knew where there was carbon paper in a drawer in the house. He had a fair hand at printing letters, although his long-hand was unreadable. In fact, it couldn't be remotely referred to a long-hand, more as scribble.

He found and lifted a sheet of plain white paper approximately twelve inches long by eight-and-a-half inches wide and placed it on the kitchen table in front of him, before sitting down. He carefully folded it in half and placed a sheet of carbon inside. He ruled a horizontal cross line an inch down from the top of the page, in pencil. He'd discounted using pens, because he couldn't pressure the nib without it buckling, but he could press down hard with a pencil, the impression going down and through the carbon.

Then he laboriously printed a heading above the line reading: 'St John's News' and stared at it deep in concentration for a minute or so.

Needed something else? Besides a date, of course and whatever else?

Some kind of Latin inscription, to give the transcript some strength?

A touch of maturity, p'raps?

It was staring him in the face!

The RAF moto: Per Ardua ad Astra (Through adversity to the Stars)

Smash-n'-grab their motto?

Well, he decided, just part of it

AD ASTRA!

That was a start.

Over the next week, after scanning local newspapers to get the drift of topical content and what was needed, he came to the realisation that he couldn't do it all by himself. This set him to thinking about who he could approach at school, to join him in his venture?

He had a major hurdle in that he needed the school's blessing to get it off the ground. That buffer assumed the form of 'Dixie'. If he started passing out sheets around the school, it would soon get to the Head's eyes-n'-ears and without some sort of authority or permission, it could all go pear-shaped. He had to give that subject some serious scalp-scratching.

Contents must be newsy and local, he nodded to himself, and should draw the attention of readers like history of St Johns, thinking about the school's archives, names of teachers working there, but without the student nicknames for them, which was a NO-NO! He could write about and cover the coming lantern-light lectures, which were normally posted on the school bulletin board in the hall. There were the football team fixtures list and name of selected players, but this could be contentious at best! A simple crossword puzzle and he knew in his mind's eye, the very lad for that.

Mechanics of producing it would be to try pencil printing through three single sheets of folded white paper. Done three times, and the production run would amount to a massive dozen sheets for distribution.

The following day, he sidled up to the crossword 'king', with an artificial smile. He was immediately regarded with grave suspicion, so he had to use his extensive gift-of-the-gab ability to even get him to listen, let alone, win him over. To his relief, he managed it and the bookish loner agreed to draw up an easy crossword for the first issue. Another of his school friends, who fortunately was also what some might call a 'mucker' of the September Road crowd, was tentatively obliging in helping out on the hand printing side. However, both boys were only lukewarm on the subject, and only consented to join 'for a laugh!'.

First bash at an initial issue ran to two folded sheets of white paper, presenting four pages, which he'd finally produced after hours of sweated toil and lip-biting. Now it was up to him to try and approach the Headmaster and sell him on the project?

No easy matter.

After a great deal of more thought, he decided that the best way to get Dixie's attention, was to 'ambush' him in the school corridor. 'Course, this manufactured its own problems, like absenting himself from class with the dreamed-up excuse 'got to go to the toilet, sir', but then he'd hover near the Head's door to his office in the corridor, but which might just go belly-up, if he was spotted by another pupil who would naturally jump to the immediate conclusion that he'd been sent to the Head for punishment? Or, alternatively, if another teacher happened in the corridor, might just question him as to what he was doing loitering there, instead of being at his desk, in class?

Nothing, but nothing, he despaired, was easy in this world!

He groaned, apprehensively.

As luck would have it, he did manage to intercept the Head scurrying into view and in a hurry as usual, arriving at his office door, hand already on the knob and beginning to turn it to gain entry.

The Head in a hurry was not a surprise, because he not only ran the school, but also participated in taking classes when there no other teachers available. Here, there and everywhere!

Dixie didn't wave him off, did pause to listen, and was patient. Dixie frowned to understand what it was the boy was trying to tell him, as the lad stood and blurted out his impromptu reason, unused to presenting a plan.

He breathlessly explained to the Head, disclosed in a rush of clumsily fumbled words, the outline details of his publishing venture, even though he experienced difficulty in marshalling his facts in progressive order, but presenting a specimen copy – held in air – to back up his poor explanation.

The Head's reaction was to give him a quick smile, patted him on the shoulder and plucked the hand-written news-sheet from his hand.

He said to come back to his office immediately after classes were concluded for the day, with his two 'colleagues' in tow, so that they could discuss the whole project in more detail.

Dixie then disappeared through the doorway into his office, the door closing on the lone figure in the corridor, who by this time was bursting with personal satisfaction and was over the moon!

**War News!**

- RAF Mosquito fighter-bombers successfully raid Gestapo Headquarters at Aarhus University, Denmark

# 19. Boys Who?

The field was a mud patch and almost unplayable with their regular football or 'casey' as they'd always called it. The leather ball, when it was wet after rain, seemed to be twice its weight. If he was required to head the ball from a corner or at close quarters, it was like heading a cannonball – well, it almost knocked his head off. Leastways, he'd blink and see stars, and he got a mini-headache afterwards, which meant he'd try to avoid heading the casey, whenever he could. Didn't seem to bother some of the boys, but it bothered him, and that was enough and sufficient reason to make sure he wasn't in a position to have to. Also, he was aware that he was given 'stick' by the rest of the team if he failed to head the ball correctly. Any claim that it gave him a headache, would be brushed aside contemptuously.

Gossip, on September Road amongst the lads, had it that there were vacancies to be had to join some youth church group or whatever, at Holy Trinity on Breck Road. Also, it was said, they had pretty good junior and senior gymnast teams who were always in competition. That they had a band also, for those musicaly inclined types. Well, he reasoned, he liked physical sports and was musical – kind of?

It was one of his classmates who had all the 'gen' about this BB company, he'd heard about.

"Boys what?" he asked the other kid in the school playground, during the mid-morning break.

"Twenty-Third Company, Boys Brigade."

"That what you belong to?"

"Twenty-Third," the boy repeated.

"Where's that?"

"Holy Trinity Church on Breck Road."

"In the church?"

"No, under it. There's a basement, where we meet."

He stared back, thinking about it.

The other boy added. "Somewhere to go at night, during the week. An' you get a uniform, too."

"I was in the Cubs, for a while," he informed the other lad, vaguely, indifferently as an aside. "Would that be alright?"

"Not like the Scouts. It's different," the other told him.

"You said, a uniform?"

"Round pillbox hat." The lad smiled back, raising both hands to the top of his head in circular motion. "White haversack and a leather belt with the BB logo that reads 'Sure & Steadfast' on the brass buckle."

He paused again, for a moment, to take it in. After a further second or two, said. "Yeah. I think I've seen them marching around," trying to recall, just where?

"That's right. We have a parade once a month," the lad volunteered.

"What else?"

"Sports. We got two teams – seniors and juniors."

This sparked his interest and his mind sat up and took notice.

"You in the sports?"

"The team, you mean?"

"Whatever?"

"Naw! Not interested in sports," was the lad's reply.

He didn't take him up on that response, but mentally was perplexed and couldn't understand why this boy – or any boy – would not be interested in sports?

"They got other things, like card games, draughts, darts…Oh, they got a band section, as well."

"Sounds okay," he laughed, but the other lad didn't recognise his weak pun. He opined that the winter nights were taking their toll on his outside activities and narrowing his options and interests; then added, off chance. "When you going up there, next?"

"Tonight. Why? D'you wanna come?"

He let his head loll to one side, before replying, weighing it up. "Yeah! Why not?"

"D'you want me to come to yours?"

He nodded.

"'Bout quart-to-seven, yeah?" the lad ventured, brightening up at the prospect.

He nodded firmly.

His mum's brothers had belonged to that Company at Holy Trinity Parish Church, Walton Breck, when they were lads, so she'd told him, and when they lived in Abbey Road, just off Townsend Lane. 'Course, they were his grown-up uncles, married and with families of their own and living elsewhere in Liverpool. All three of his uncles were now in the army and serving overseas. One was in the British Eighth Army, who had recently been fighting and defeating Rommel in the North African deserts.

He gave the idea some thought. The winter was dragging on, which limited the number of dry days, when the boys could meet on the corner of the road to play-out the latest cowboy film they'd seen or for the odd game of footie, it forced him to think of other pursuits. Seemed like, not only to him, but to the rest of his crowd, that it rained just about every other day. Sun rarely showed its face. Then, of course, the winter days grew shorter and the daylight time got less and less.

A right bore!

So he ended up meeting a boy from his class, who told him about Holy Trinity's BB Company at the junction of Richmond Park and Walton Breck, and got him vaguely interested in the first place, but he was unsure about what he might be getting himself involved with? This was always a major consideration in all his thinking, with him. He'd be presenting and maybe involving himself in something that didn't suit him?

He recalled his earlier experience with the Boy Scouts when he was a Cub, but that hadn't lasted long, even though he'd had the cap bought for him and he'd even managed the 'tenderfoot' badge. Again, that was because not enough was going on.

His school friend came by the house, but didn't knock, and stood outside on the pavement, loitering. He saw, from his position behind the curtain at his front bedroom window, the boy's arrival at the gate. Saw also, that he wore his white haversack across his right shoulder and down across his dark jacket, held in place by a leather belt, the white pressed baggy portion handing neatly at his left side. The boy's 'pill box' round BB hat was held firmly under his left jacket armpit, securely against the side of his skinny chest.

Out on the pavement and making their way to the BB meeting, they entered into earnest animated chat about the organisation. He asked all the questions that came immediately to mind, which his school chum attempted to immediately reply to and others he was only vaguely aware of.

Yes, the BB was started a long, long time ago.

"When was that?" he asked.

"Dunno, just yonks ago?"

"Where did it start up?" he then asked, thinking of Baden Powell and the Boy Scout movement.

"Phew! Up in Scotland, I think?"

"So, how long has the BB been at Holy Trinity?" was another question, choosing not to tell the boy his mum-n'-dad had married there, so his mum had remarked when he'd told her where he was going that evening, and why.

"Before the war."

"Which one?"

"This one – oh, yeah! Not the Great War."

The entrance to the 23$^{rd}$ BB meeting hall was through the side wall of the Church garden's surround, on Richmond Park road. A descending path led to the rooms and compartments beneath the church. A sort of expanding cellar or cellars. There seemed to be plenty of activity, with boys rushing around enjoying and chasing each other, He also noted that they were attired in the BB 'uniform' of leather belt and buckle, which exhibited the 'Sure & Steadfast' logo, and a white over-the-shoulder white linen haversack. Their 'pillbox' head-gear with the number '23' prominent and polished, shone brightly on the front, but were being carried temporarily underarm as they played 'tick' and other chase games, prior to the night's start-up.

A smartly dressed and officious man in his fifties, addressed as 'Captain' called the boys to order. The excitable voices and laughter breathlessly ceased as they took up a sort of congregated group around and in front of the senior officer. The leader had all the outward presence of being very efficient and in charge, waving them to him with a trace of a smile, showing on his red-complexioned clean-shaven features.

"Boys…boys, let's settle down. Now form into the usual two lines in front of me, left arm extended out from the shoulder of the lad next to you, heels together, shuffle into line, there…shuffle. Smartly does it! C'mon now!"

His friend left him standing just inside the spacious room cellar-area below Holy Trinity Church building, where other BB members were congregating and generally chatting before they were called to order. Some twenty or so boys, not the whole company, he had been assured, came together in the centre of the floor, forming into two ragged ranks, sorting and shuffling about to form orderly straight lines, all carried out as efficiently as possible, with a minimum of fuss and murmurings.

The CO called out for the formation to 'Right Dress', which had the two lines of boys shooting out the left arm level with the shoulder to touch the shoulder of the lad next to him and twisting the head around to look right, so that even spaces were activated between each boy.

"Arms down!" the captain ordered. "And that means yours arms straight down and flat against your sides, and fingers pressed firmly onto the seams of your trousers."

The group fidgeted to carry out the command, with some even glancing down to ensure they'd got it right.

"Eyes front! I didn't give the order to look down to see where your arms and fingers were touching," barked their commander.

The odd head snapped back silently.

"At ease!" he finally said, followed by, "Stand easy!" which had some boys moving their shoulders, bending knees in an exaggerated fashion, as though relieved after standing at attention for hours!

The boys in the under-church hall space knew the drill and were soon conforming, re-fitting their pill-boxes in place on their heads, stepping into line with each other, staring along their raised left arms, connecting to the boys next to them.

"Your arms should all be down at your side, eyes front! Smartly, now!"

There was a concentrated effect at efficient conformity and the corresponding slap of limbs briskly falling into position against their sides.

"Keep your positions! Attention!"

Then, "Rear Ranks, one step backward march!" the Captain ordered, as he stepped forward to inspect the ranks, his commander's baton thrust firmly under his left arm.

He roamed slowly and silently along in front of the silent statues, examining each boy's uniformed turnout, carefully. His eyes searched down to check that their footwear had been polished to a shine, that their socks had been pulled up tidily to below the knees, clean shirt buttoned up to the neck with a dark tie knotted in place. His eyes also sought out the position of the pillboxes and corrected those that: (a) had a quiff protruding and showing from under the front of the headdress, or (b) not being firmly sited squarely on top of the head and some with the pillbox at a jaunty angle.

Joining or enrolling in the BB, didn't present any problems, except he had to go through the steps of being presented to the CO or Captain of the Twenty-Third Company.

From his position just inside the entrance, awaiting his introduction to the Captain, he watched and could see instantly that two dozen or so boys of varying ages were as one in enjoying the discipline of the assembly. Nobody was forced into becoming a member of the BB, and he could tell by their facial expressions that they completely enjoyed the joy and pleasure of being part of this activity.

Of belonging!

They were all striving to comply and to please.

"At ease!"

After inspection, the Captain spoke a few words of congratulation at the turnout and then proceeded to read from a sheet of paper, outlining plans for the week's coming events, including the monthly church parade on the forthcoming Sunday, after church services. Judging by the sea of smiles and natural reaction, this was the icing-on-the cake on the ladder of rituals performed.

The Captain's short address over, the evening's parade was stood to attention again and then dismissed, releasing the lads to join their respective groups, some headed off at a gallop out of the building and down Richmond Park to the school, where the sports section practised and performed.

There was some brief comings-and-goings of officers wanting a word with the Captain before they dispersed and hurried away to their duties.

He watched keenly from the doorway, taking it all in, as these orderly commands followed by departing movements, were attended. He liked what he saw: the semi-military stance and approach and automatic response to commands.

The captain's tone of voice eased to a gentle and kindly smoothness, as he greeted them quietly and wished them a 'good-evening', before consulting some hand-written notes on a sheet of paper held in his left hand. He spoke to the boys about what subjects were being addressed, that evening. He further added his own comments and informed all attending that the following Sunday would be a march-past and parade after morning service. He added a further comment about tardiness and the importance of punctuality and added 'better late than never!'.

The formation was dismissed and his friend waved him forward, from his position by the entrance door so that he could be formally introduced to the captain. He stepped smartly forward as he saw his friend speaking confidentially to the captain and pointing in his direction. As he strode forward, he mentally reflected that he'd made an effort to be presentable wearing a dark tie in place at the collar of his clean shirt. Had recently had his hair cut, which was now flattened down, combed-n'-brushed flat, kept in place with copious amounts of 'corporation hair oil' or tap water to most of his mates.

Finally, he – as a visitor and enlistee – was led by his school chum and introduced to the Captain.

"So you're…?" he questioned, turning to eye the visitor with a friendly smile and a right hand thrust forward for a firm warm handshake.

"Yessir!" he replied with accompanying grin, returning the hand-shake.

"Well…" The company commander leaned forward, bending slightly to him, looking first at his introductory school chum and then to him.

"I s'pose he's told you what we expect and what we get from all of our boys: that they look neat and tidy and wearing dark clothing, nice, neat haircut brushed firmly back – like yours-" he noticed. "Dark or preferably black shoes, highly polished, for starters?"

"Yes, sir!"

"And deportment, bearing and general behaviour should be displayed at all times. In other words, the same respect and exemplary conduct shown by the boys here tonight. Think you can do that?"

"Yes, sir!"

"Good," the captain said, straightening up and patting him on the shoulder.

"Well, you'd better let your friend take you over to our quarter master to fill out all the appropriate forms and to kit you out. Alright?"

"Yes, sir!"

The interview was over and he'd been accepted. The rest of this, his first evening, was given over to signing forms, receiving his kit with instructions on how it should be worn and tips on cleaning brasses, etc. Later, he was introduced to more of the regular members of the 23$^{rd}$ BB Company.

On his way home, afterwards, carrying his 'uniform' in a loaned cloth bag, he experienced elated euphoria. Then the thought struck him that he hadn't said he'd be joining tonight! That worry soon dismissed, because – after all – weren't her brothers all in the BB when they were young? He reckoned she'd be pleased, and so reassured by this line of reasoning. He looked forward to surprising her.

**War News!**

- British Home Guard is disbanded and officially stood down.

# 20. Holy Mother Church

There was a religious hour, each week, at St John's school, as and because it was part of St John the Baptist Church on the corner of West Derby Road and Green Lane, Tuebrook. And, as happens, just opposite one of his 'Temple of Dreams', the Carlton Picture House.

This subject always took the first school hour between nine and ten o'clock with the top class. Usually, one of the assistant priest's would attend and would be responsible for religious instruction during that hour.

He found the priest's attitude somewhat disturbing, during religious instruction, because the priest was insistent on the pupil's close attention at all times, when he was explaining the meaning of a selected section of the Bible, old or new testament. It became immediately clear to him that one particular priest, aged in his early thirties, and always – it seemed to him – on a short fuse, didn't take kindly to muttered conversation among pupils in class, whilst he was in the middle of an explanation of his interpretation of what religious studies was all about.

To emphasise his insistence, it was not unusual for him to pick up and throw a heavy wood-backed blackboard duster in the direction of the distraction. Either he wasn't very practised in his aim or only intended to dramatically exhibit his irritation, but the priest never actually hit anybody with the missile, during the time he attended, that is. The action, certainly, focussed the heads-up attention of the secret whisperers. This particular priest always gave the impression that he had not volunteered to take the class in religious instruction. This was evidenced when at the end of his instruction, he'd ask the class for 'any questions?'. There never were any. Or, let it be said, that if someone had hazarded to respond, he might end up being humiliated, being the focus of ridicule. Further, he might be accused of not listening closely or intently enough to what was being said. Better, most decided, was to stay silent. This, he decided, recalling his Sunday School days during his evacuation during the Blitz, and was not anything approaching comparison with his lovely memories of Warton.

Come Sunday, and he and another boy out of his class, did attend the High Mass service at eleven o'clock, sharp. It wasn't something he normally did, but then his mum and dad were not regular church-goers, and so there was not the discipline in place to attend service. It was not a subject that he was ever concerned with, and only now became apparent as a result of the religious instruction hour at St John's school.

As he approached the red sandstone edifice, he couldn't fail to notice it's size, against the diminutive white concrete slabbed Martins Bank building, nearby.

Once inside, his eyes roamed the spaces, seeing a central aisle at the end of which was the sanctuary and beyond, the high altar, above which was a large, tall brilliantly colourful east window, showing leading figures of the faith in a collection of still glass-leaded pictures.

The church was already pretty full, so he and his classmate were happy to slide into a back wooden pew.

Kneeling to mentally recite a personal respectful prayer, his eyes once more roved around and picked up the statue figure of Our Lady, just in front and before the entrance on the left to the Lady Chapel. Around the inner walls were the fourteen Stations of the Cross.

Finally, the senior priest appeared, joined by his 'assistant priests and several boys in white surplices, approaching and ascending the steps to the High Altar. He recognised some of the boys in their loose vestments from his class but were not personal friends.

Mum didn't ask where he'd been. He was trusted and given free rein, most times. His mum had just assumed he'd gone to the field to play with his mates, so she was quite taken aback and surprised when he sat at the table for Sunday lunch and told her he'd been to church!

"Church? – Oh, you mean Holy Trinity?"

"No, St John the Baptist."

She raised a questioning eyebrow but continued to lay the table.

"What made you want to go there?"

"The priest told us we should go. Besides, it is St John the Baptist church, which belongs to our school, you know, Mum."

"Which priest?" she paused.

"The one at school who takes us for religious instruction."

"Don't you mean, the minister?"

"No," he said, hardly fazed and matter-of-factly.

"The minister?" she pressed.

"The priest."

"Didn't know they had priests…It is a Protestant church, isn't it?" she paused again.

"'Course!" he told her.

Dad looked up from his *Sunday People* newspaper. "Some Protestant churches call their clergy priests."

"I've never heard of that before. I attended regular church before we were married."

Dad added by way of explanation. "It's a High Church of England, which is close to the Roman Catholic church. There's a lot of similar traditional rules, values and similarities between the two. It's nothing new."

Mum paused to let it sink in, then said. "That church I attended, where I was born, in Preston, didn't have priests. It was always, the minister."

"That's because," Dad pointed out, "yours was a different type of Protestant church."

"I thought all Protestant churches were the same?" she responded.

"Well, no – not exactly," and continued to read his newspaper.

Mum turned her gaze back on her son.

"And he told you, you must attend church?"

He nodded back at her. "Yep. Went to High Mass with a mate from school."

"High Mass?" she repeated.

"It's what it's called."

"And what else did he tell you, you must do?"

"We sing the 'Kyrie eleison', which is the same as 'Lord, have mercy'."

"What's that 'Kyrie'…whatever?"

"Latin."

Mum just stared at him, not in any angry way, but perplexed.

"Does he want you to go to confession, too?"

Now, it was his turn to frown.

"What's confession?"

"Never mind," Mum dismissed. "Anything else?"

"Well…ah, um…he said that if St John's was full, we could just go over – 'cross the road on Green Lane, to St Cecilia's."

"St Cecilia church. That's Roman Catholic, isn't it?" she said to Dad, who just shrugged.

The subject was suddenly dropped and the Sunday dinner was carefully removed from hot pots-n'-pans on the hob and proportionately ladled onto clean wide plates.

Later, after he'd finished off his dinner or 'cleaned-his-plate' as he usually described it, he left the table to wander into the hall, intending to go upstairs.

He overheard his mum say in a hushed voice to Dad. "They didn't say anything to me about this, when I took him down to the school to register."

There followed some more muffled conversation which was not for his ears. Nothing else was said about it in the succeeding days, so – he concluded – they must've forgotten all about it.

No big deal, as far as he was concerned.

### War News!

- Elements of advancing Red Army units, together with Bulgarian People's Army and Tito's Partisan Forces,

over run and capture Belgrade, forcing the Wehrmacht into flight from the city and in general retreat.
- In the Pacific, USS Aircraft Carrier Lexington (Cv-16) 36,000 tonnes is heavily damaged after assisting the Philippine Landings, when discovered by Japanese special attack aircraft. Later, forced to return to Ulilthi for major repair.
- Essex-class American Aircraft Carrier USS Intrepid (Cv-11) is involved in the 'Battle of Leyte Gulf'. Is hit and badly damaged by Japanese Kamikaze attacks.

## 21. Next Door's Gi-Joe

"Who's the Yank livin' next door, t'ya?" one of the boys asked, casually, as the lad kicked the worn-out old tennis ball back up against the stone wall surround to a narrow front garden; then, as it rebounded, kicked it back again, before it reached the kerb edge on the road.

"What Yank?" he frowned.

"I saw him, yister'dy."

"Where?" he asked.

"Like I said, going' in through the front door of the house next to yours."

He searched for some confirmation in his memory-box, but came up with zilch, and quickly shook his head.

"News to me?"

"Hey, Kenny. You was with me, when we saw that Yank, yister'dy afternoon?"

The kid addressed, lounging against the low wall, nodded.

"There y'are, see? I wasn't lyin'."

"Didn't say you were?"

"Funny, we saw 'im, but you say you don't know nothin' about it?"

"Well," he replied, at a loss. "I don't know anything about it, but – how d'you know he was?"

"Was what?"

"A Yank. – You just said?"

"I know what I said," the lad snorted, kicking the bouncing ball yet again, back up against the wall.

Kenny spoke, "He was in an American army uniform. Had three stripes upside down, on his sleeve."

"And…" said the first lad, controlling the bouncing ball.

"What?" he asked, pacing himself as the other took his time.

"He was smoking a cigar!"

He just shook his head and smiled back in response to the comment.

Bouncing ball, then said. "Got to be a Yank, because our fellahs can't afford cigars, 'ceptin' maybe, the 'Ruperts'?"

Kenny added. "My dad sez, that's all gonna end, when this war's over."

"Oh yeah?" he invited.

"He said, the workers will take over."

"Over what?" asked Bouncy Ball, without removing his concentration.

"The – er, country. We'll get to own the railways, coal mines, steel factories, like they do in Russia. An' if we don't, there'll be a revolution."

"Gonna get rid of the King-n'-Queen?" Bouncy asked, pausing with his foot trapping the ball under the sole of his shoe, open-mouthed.

"'Course!"

"Won't happen," he interrupted.

"Why not?" Kenny queried, directing his stare, directly.

"My dad is a labour supporter, but my mum loves royalty, and she wouldn't let my dad do that. And what my mum says in our house, usually goes – gets done!"

"Yeah," agreed Bouncy, "me muther's like that, too."

They both stared back silently at Kenny: him with raised eyebrows and shrugged shoulders, in response, supporting his comment.

There was a moment of accepted silence, the full extent of their committed political intellect, completely exhausted.

"Wasn't the normal Yank," added the ball player, getting back to the original subject.

"Oh?" was all he could say, now curious himself.

"Was a coloured fellah."

He didn't say anything to that because there was nothing that came to mind.

"I haven't seen him," he finally responded, as the other two waited for some kind of comment. "Was he tall and young?"

"Short and fat. Waddled, like, rather than walked. Winked at us when we seen him passin' by. Real friendly, like."

"Why did he wink at yoos?"

"Dunno?"

"Young fellah?"

"Mm, old sort-of. Had a mussie, as well."

"Like Clark Gable?"

"No – not like Clark Gable. I jus' told yuh, he was coloured."

There was a pause while this information was digested.

"We thought – Kenny, an' me – that you might wanna share?"

"Share what?" beginning to lose the strand of the conversation.

"Chewy? – If you'd seen him, we thought – and because he was a Yank, you would've asked him, what all the kids ask Yanks: Got any gum, chum?"

He shook his head, eyes wide in puzzlement.

"That's what all the kids ask, when they meet any Yanks."

"As I've not seen this fellah in uniform, you're talking about, it's not likely I'd have asked him, yeah?"

Ball-kicker sliced the ball up on the air with the toe-poke of his left shoe, and then let rip as the ball descended hitting it with the hard instep of his right foot, sending it like a missile back against the wall with an audible THWACK!

Sat at the table, partaking evening meal, with Dad having come in from his job at the docks, and Mum already been involved with setting out the table, preparing and presenting the dinner, he sat quietly listening to his parents' small talk.

He was still ruffled by the question of his peers at the top of the road, earlier. In particular, the topic of the new resident observed going into and apparently living next door, and of whom he was totally unaware? The thing is, there wasn't much he missed, so their comments were doubly disturbing and stung.

It occurred to him to ask his mum, because she seemed to be in the know about who, what and why of everybody locally, as opposed to his dad, who didn't seem too interested in who came and went in the neighbourhood. His dad would leave all that sort of know-how up to Mum, who would inform and p'raps discuss the subject with him. There again, maybe they'd already chattered about it, up at the pub, when they spent an hour or so over drinks, after evening repast?

Certainly, his internal radar, in the form of eavesdropping around the house, hadn't produced any indication in that field. He accepted he was a nosey bugger, and usually didn't miss a trick, but somehow, this knowledge had slipped past his personal radar unnoticed, and it bothered him, because he liked to be aware and on top of everything going on around him, and which would be of interest to him. Not to be, was slightly alarming, in that his sensitivities were clearly slipping in that direction, somewhat?

Normally, he was away from the dinner table, within seconds of finishing off his scoff: (a) because there was just the chance he could avoid being asked by Mum to clear away, wash-n'-dry the dishes, which she would occasionally ask him to do and which he never refused or moaned about, and (b) because their conversation was mostly about mundane matters, which were a tad boring to say the least.

This particular evening, he delayed his usual rush away from the table, just in case they happened to mention the new boarder, next door?

When it became clear to him, that this wasn't a subject they were about to talk about, he decided to remove himself from the table.

"No homework, tonight?" Mum asked casually looking in his direction.

"Done it, already."

"Oh well, in that case, you wouldn't mind clearing the table for me?" she said, standing up and yawning.

Dad added, "Polish my shoes for morning, will you, China?" followed by a smile and explanation. "Been a tiring day."

He smiled artificially back and nodded in the face of the double whammy. Upon reflection, he realised it wasn't too much to ask him to do, considering what they did for him.

He made quick work of both chores and blamed himself for bringing them on. Should've been faster off the mark – or burst out of the chocks sooner, using sports parlance.

Later, stood just behind the window curtain in his upstairs front bedroom, he stared down at the scene below, where the short separate paved paths from the road served and led to the steps up to each front door. Normally, he wouldn't have bothered to stand there, but his curiosity had got the better of him. It was rapidly getting dark, when he saw movement beyond, but close to, the hedge of next door's front garden. Suddenly, the uniformed figure of the burly American soldier stepped into view as he crossed the threshold from the pavement onto next door's front path. The soldier, short in stature, but broad of shoulder and inclined to be tubby, looking – he guessed – to be a couple of years older that his big brother, or thereabout, was very dark skinned. The soldier glanced up quickly at the bedroom windows of the houses. He hurriedly ducked down and away from the upstairs front window, to avoid being seen.

So, the kids were right!

Must be new?

A recent boarder?

Couldn't get it out of his head that he thought all soldiers lived in tents or something – didn't they, he asked himself? Didn't know of any British Tommies who lived in houses, 'cepting their own, when they was on leave!

At the dinner table, the following evening, he waited for his parents to finish eating, before raising the object of his curiosity.

"Ah…there's an American soldier staying next door, did you know?"

"That's right," Mum replied, which threw him, because she'd never spoken about it, so he had concluded it would come as a complete surprise?

He was taken aback, momentarily. Especially, at the fact that his mum knew and he didn't!

"Your dad had a word with him, the other night over a pint, in the pub."

That shook him!

Seemed like everybody and his brother knew of the stranger taking up residence next door, 'cept him!

"No barracks?" he asked.

Dad looked up from his newspaper and supplied part of an answer. "Working on the docks, checking American merchant ship bills-of-lading, arriving and unloading supplies and equipment…" And then added when he saw the confusion on his son's face. "Checking what's unloaded against the ship's manifests. – clerical duties, in other words. So he's probably been authorised expenses to cover his stay in billeted civilian rented accommodation, while he's assigned here."

That was a lot for him to take in and he had to think about it, but a great source of ancillary information which he'd use to impress the other kids in the road.

Couple of days later, he finished his dinner at tea-time and decided to meet up with his mates at the top of the road for a chin-wag or to drift along to Pop's sweet shop on the corner of July and Lower Breck road, where he'd play the pin-ball machine. He liked that, because he was fascinated with building up a score as the ball bearings struck home on the electric bollards and racked up a score, bells ringing, lights popping and then numbers thudding up on the counter. Sometimes he'd high-score and the bells would ring out louder, rewarding him with extra games. In fact, he was so obsessed with playing the machine, that his mates would give up trying to get him to leave off and depart.

"Just one more go?" he'd plead.

"We're goin'," they'd say to his back, exasperated.

"Look! LOOK! – I'm into a big score!"

Until he'd physically wrestle too much with machine, lifting it slightly, until it suddenly froze to a sudden stop, flashing the dreaded word TILT! to his disgust.

It was time to head back home, with darkness descending and the other boys parting ways, one by one, peeling off to go indoors.

It was about that time he'd shouted his goodbyes with the last pal, and alone, he headed out of the Entry, made his way across the road to the front gate entrance to his own house.

He stepped through before he realised he had company and looked up to find the coloured GI in company with a woman on his arm, whom he didn't recognise, but looked to be about his mother's age, except that she had a lot of that paint-n'-powder women apply to their faces with a fox fur wrap, like his late gran's, wound around her neck.

"Hello duckie!" she greeted him, smiling pleasantly, while her companion in uniform just stared down blankly at him, but holding open the front door, for which she said. "Thank you, Joe, you're a gentleman."

"H-hello," he half-heartedly responded, because normally grown-up strangers didn't address kids like him.

They were gone in through the front door, shutting it firmly behind them.

He stopped for a moment, before fitting his front door key into the lock, Dad and Mum being up the road, at this time.

Questions queued up to be answered:

Didn't he have any GI friends?

Was that his mother? – Couldn't be, 'cause she was white.

Was it, maybe, a girl friend?

Was it...somebody's else's girl friend?

He didn't really understand any of it, 'specially grown-up relationships.

And why soldiers had to have a woman friend, anyways?

And this fellah, like his dad said, doing an important job down on the docks, supervising the unloading of all those supplies sent over from the USA for the American army in Britain?

All very involved and complex?

He shoved the key into the lock, turned it and thrust open the front door.

The following evening, about the same time, as he was stepping down September Road and close to turning to walk onto the path of his house, to his wide-eyed surprised met the couple, leaving their front door.

They almost brushed arms in passing. He found himself suddenly gawping as the black soldier in American Army uniform turned his head, stared back down and caught his inquisitive gaze as the couple passed him by. Just as instantly, the uniform winked; then grinned in such an infectious friendly way his nosey curiosity was at once disarmed.

He immediately, sheepishly responded and instantly returned the smile.

## War News

- Allied troops commence series of amphibious landings against German defensive positions in the flooded Scheldt Estuary. Fierce fighting ensued as they faced stoutly defended enemy strong points. This operation, was considered very necessary in order to clear the approaches to and in the port of Antwerp, in order for the Allied armies thrusting deep into enemy lines in Northern Belgium and France, could be speedily and successfully supplied.
- Naval convoy success rates of Arctic convoys to Russian ports improved immeasurably, with no vessels lost during the months of October and November 1944, it was disclosed via Security summaries.
- German forces (Wehrmacht) gather and launch a massive strike against Allied columns steadily advancing on all fronts toward German frontier with Belgium and France. Route of plan is through the wooded Ardennes, with its aim of re-taking and occupying the port of Antwerp.

# 22. Harmonies and Helmets at the Christmas Party

"Party?" his voice reaching a higher tone, as both ears simultaneously shot up at the same time at the mention of such an unusual event. This was whilst he was sat at the dinner table one weekday evening and where most of the main issues affecting the house, and him in particular, got aired and discussed.

"Christmas Party. – Just a quiet affair, you understand," Mum explained. "Not family, because most are overseas. More," Mum strained slightly to spell out. "More like friends of your dad and Mrs Sherry and her…"

"V coming?"

"Of course, if she wants to, that is. If she's not working and it's her night off?"

"Uncle Jim, as well?"

"Yes," Mum replied, collecting the dinner plates after they'd finished eating.

"Dad's friends?"

"One or two of his workmates, so to speak, and…ah…" Mum's sentence, fading off as she paused and turned in Dad's direction looking for him to fill in the blanks.

"Jim's associates at the station," he added.

"Police station?" big ears, repeated.

"No…No," Dad corrected. "Central Station in town."

"Other scuffers?" he blurted with mounting excitement.

"Don't you mean 'policemen'?" Mum frowned back at him.

He shrugged, but then amended his words. "Police."

"Well, not exactly," Dad supplied.

It was Mum's turn to look uncertainly at Dad. "Not, policemen?"

"Sort of," Dad grinned.

Mum and he both started back at Dad, nonplussed.

"Well, they're military police," he supplied, and as an afterthought. "American."

His little-boy face lit up like a beacon. "Really?"

Dad shrugged. "According to Jim, just a couple of American colleagues attached to Central, the Railway Station, just down from Lime Street – the Adelphi."

He was still beaming as Mum went on to explain that it would be this coming Friday night, and that it would probably go on past his bedtime, but that didn't mean he could stay up or anything like that. After all, she told him, it was a small adults get-together sort of cum-Christmas party."

A thought immediately struck him. "Does that include the coloured sergeant from next door, and his…" he almost said, 'fancy lady' but didn't. A term the kids in the road had picked up, also after eavesdropping on his parent's chit-chat, a week or so, earlier.

"No," Mum replied, "that soldier works down on the ships and the warehouses and has nothing to do with the MPs at Central Station. They wouldn't know him."

No matter, he was tickled-pink over the arrangement, especially as he'd get to meet them and then, later, to tell all his cronies in the road all about it!

Late, Friday afternoon, unusual items and articles began appearing on the kitchen table in the form of rectangular 'Devonshire' loaves, packets of margarine and the 'makings' in the form of spam. On the back kitchen floor, there were brown-coloured unopened beer bottles grouped like soldiers on parade, but in uneven ranks. He stared at it all and scratched his head to wonder where his mum had managed to scrape together all this lot? But then, he understood, most people – and he'd heard it said, over and over again – were very resourceful during the war.

Mum arrived home early from work and immediately set to and started on making the sandwiches for that evening's party. He watched her closely, as she worked swiftly and purposely, stacking and slicing them into manageable sections, placing them carefully – again, in stacks – on clean white crockery, draping tea-towels over them before storing the plates in the pantry cupboard.

He watched her work silently and with confident intent, and his mouth watered at the thought of her inviting layout of soft fresh bread and spam, one of his favourite munchies.

His dad came in through the front door about this time carrying a heavily laden linen bag, whose contents he unloaded onto the kitchen table, and included – what looked like to him – and was confirmed when he read the label, as whisky, rum and port.

"Haven't forgotten you, China," Dad said to him, a smile on his smirking friendly face, lifting two bottles of lemonade from the bottom of the bag, the line of bubbles clearly seen on the inside at the neck of each bottle, disturbed by passage and movement, and by his eager searching lively brown eyes.

Mrs Sherry and V knocked on the front door about seven-ish, were quickly let in and welcomed by Mum with warm genuine Yule-tide greetings. A cuppa for each being hurriedly prepared: kettle of cold fresh water brought to the boil and then poured onto the contents of several spoonfuls of tea leaves from the caddy into one of Mum's large brown teapots; then drenched with hot, but not boiling water, lid replaced and left to brew for a couple of minutes, as the tea infused to produced the flavoured non-bitter taste and rich nutty-brown colour, before being poured into shiny-clean china tea cups, when – and only then, milk being added…and sugared, if required.

This was how his mum made a nice cup of tea, he had often observed, and he saw how she took pains-n'-effort in doing so, to produce the cuppa of perfection.

'Course, some folks have a sweet tooth, so one or two full or level teaspoonfuls of sugar might be added?

'Course, if it was left up to him, but more to the point, if it was FOR him? Yes, well, with nobody watching, three heaped spoonfuls of sugar, you betcha!

From the kitchen, he heard a knocking and ran-tan at the front door, which Mum answered. Upstairs in his bedroom, his ears picked up the murmur and shrill laughter of visitors, followed by heavy footsteps over the vestibule tiled floor, into the hallway and finally, the muffled friendly voices, interrupted by more laughter, from the front room.

He shot downstairs and into the kitchen. His curiosity knew no bounds.

Mum appeared in the kitchen and had Dad go to the front room to find out what they all might like to drink? There was a lull in the conversation and then Dad reappeared, reaching for a tray in passing and collecting some glasses before continuing into the back kitchen, selecting a couple of bottled beers from the floor and also a bottle of port, which he took out with him, when he returned to the people assembled in the sitting room.

"D'you want me to stay out of the sitting room?" he asked Mum.

"What?" she answered him absentmindedly.

"D'you want me not to go in to see those people who've just come?" he rephrased, trying not to be a nuisance or get in the way of this early evening activity.

"I didn't say that," Mum protested, suddenly aware of what he'd asked.

"No, I know you didn't," he agreed.

"Yes, by all means, go and mingle with them. Make yourself acquainted," then as an afterthought. "Here, fill that glass up on the table with lemonade or dandelion-n'-burdock, and take it with you."

He quickly filled a small tumbler with lemonade, drank a good mouthful, swallowed, then proceeded to refill the glass to the very top.

He was as inquisitive as could be because it sounded like the Americans had arrived with Uncle Jim.

"Gosh a'mighty!" he heard one over-the-pond voice exclaim. "You got gas lighting – no electricity, huh?"

"No yet," he heard Dad reply.

"Reminds me of that movie 'Gaslight' with Ingrid Bergman and Charles Boyer…"

A woman's voice interrupted. "It's called 'The Murder in Thornton Square' over here."

"Oh, right!" said the American visitor. "Somebody gotten murdered in the house in London, and years later her niece or something, returns with this Italian guy…"

Woman's voice interrupts again. "Ingrid Bergan had fallen in love with Charles Boyer and they returned to London, on'y she doesn't know he was the murderer of her aunt who usta live there, but had to scarper at the time and was unable to steal her aunt's jewellery – which, is what he was after all the time…"

"And," added the American, "didn't he try to make out she was nuts or something', like saying he'd lost his watch, an' then they found it in her handbag, an' all the time he was…"

"That's right," the woman's voice agreed. "Her aunt's belongings had been stored in the attic, so every night Boyer left the house, but doubled back to sneak up into the attic and search through the belongings for the aunt's jewellery…"

"Jeeze!" the American continued. "Doesn't he frighten the be-jazus out of her, by lighting the gas mantles in the attic, which scares the poor woman's wits outta her, sat downstairs, especially when the gaslight in her parlour dims every time Boyer lights up the one in the attic!"

"That's right!" squeals the female voice again, in agreement.

All exciting chat to his young ears and he couldn't get in there quick enough, 'specially as he'd seen that picture, too. And, yes, it had scared the daylights out of him, as well!

He meticulously filled his glass to the very top, yet again, even to it starting to leak over the rim, so that he was forced to place mouth to glass, asap, to prevent wastage, and dripping liquid on lino and carpet.

"D'you think you could get any more lemo in your glass?" Dad joked, as the overspill began to dribble and run down the outside. If he hadn't had to pause to turn Dad's way, when he spoke to him, it wouldn't have happened. However, his gripping fingers caught and trapped the overspill and he was double quick to change hands, holding the glass, and to lick the tasty nectar from his wet freed fingers.

The front room was alive with noise generated by adults seated and standing and in earnest happy conversation. Already a smoky fuzz was forming from lit cigarettes, held firmly between thumbs and forefingers, and used sometimes to emphasise a point or two, in the friendly interchange of chit-chat.

Someone had brought along an electric record player and even now, the noise levels had risen as talkers raised their voice in competition or challenged by the music filling the room.

On entering the room, he was immediately recognised as the host's 'little boy' and warmly greeted and fussed. However, the first thing he noticed were one policeman's helmet and two American army white military police garrison caps grouped together at one end of the upright piano top. Uncle Jim was in boisterous good humour, with the two military policemen, both of whom wore black arm brassards with letters 'MP' in white. Close by was Mrs Sherry next to her burly husband, holding a small glass of port, which she sipped at from time to time. Uncle Jim emptied his brown bottle of dark beer into a glass he was holding, quaffing half the contents in one big gulp, seemed like to him, watching on, while the Americans drank light golden whatever from small glasses. On the floor between them, was a large bottle of similar coloured liquid, with the word Bourbon showing on the printed label of the bottle.

Suddenly, his young eyes lit up as he spied a crumpled untidy mess of military equipment in the corner of the room, which drew him onto it immediately. He could see a US army belt with what looked like a brown wood baseball bat attached, also a set of handcuffs. He was still staring down at them when an American voice, which had snook up behind him, said at his shoulder.

"You wanna hold it?"

He whirled about, wide-eyed. "Is that a…" he said point down.

"Baton? Sure, here," said the speaker, reaching down to remove the baton from its holder, and handing it to him.

He held it in his hands and examined it closely, as if it was an alien relic from a space ship, turning it over in his hands and sliding his fingers over the polished wood, moving up to the hand grip.

"Wow!" was all he could say, into the grinning face of the US army military policeman.

"Try mine," Uncle Jim interrupted, passing his railway police baton for him to hold.

Right away, he noticed the difference. For one, it was black, like ebony wood, and was almost twice as heavy in his hands, even though it was much smaller in length.

"Well?" Uncle Jim smirked.

"Heavy – heavier," he corrected.

"That's because it has a lead core," his uncle explained.

Now, he held both separately in each hand and marvelled at their touch.

Mum's face suddenly appeared before him.

"No, you can't take them out in the road to show your mates," she laughed.

Uncle Jim said. "Didn't you used to go to piano lessons?"

He paused before answering.

Mum answered for him. "Yes, of course, you did."

Uncle Jim then said. "So, play us a tune, why don't you?"

"I don't know…" he almost stammered, very hesitant and caught off guard.

"C'mon kid, let's see what you can do?" the military policeman urged, stepping aside so he could go sit on the stool at the piano.

"I'm not sure?" he tried again, hoping to back out of the request.

Seconds later, Dad was there alongside Mum.

"Play us that tune I've heard you play a few times, over the past week?"

"I…I don't have any sheet music."

"I didn't see any sheet music on the piano, when you were playing?"

"C'mon, let's hear it?" the smiling American joined in.

He almost cringed in embarrassment and found himself steered across the room to the empty piano stool.

The record player was switched off in anticipation. Mum helped by lifting up the lid over the keys of the piano, and everyone in the room craned their necks and waited.

"Just the one tune," he said, apologetically.

"Fine! Let's hear it?" said Uncle Jim.

He felt himself blush. "Its…it's a funny title."

"So?"

Mum interrupted. "Just tell us the name of the song, and let us worry about how it sounds?"

"Well," he ventured in a hushed – almost an apology for a whisper – his voice turned purposely low so that the room had to reach for the words. "*You Are My Sunshine…*"

"Who sang it?" asked a voice.

"Not sure?" he replied.

"So play it?" said another.

He turned to face the keys, nervous and anxious, definitely not in his comfort zone, silently muttering in his mind 'You asked for it, so here goes'.

They were in for a big surprise…

His fingers stumbled over the first few bars, playing-by-ear and with his right hand only, because he didn't know how to vamp with his left. What reached the ears of those in the room, sounded more like a drunk tinkling the ivories, it was that unbelievably bad. Even the right hand erred by playing the wrong notes, but – and after the first stifled gasps and excited half titters – those crowded around picked up the melody and began to sing the lyrics from memory, beating out the words in loud refrain, determined to make the best of it…

*You are my sunshine, my only sunshine*
*You make me happy when skies are grey,*
*You'll never know dear, how much I love you,*
*Please don't take my sunshine away.*

Although, it was a cringe moment for him, and he felt acute embarrassment when playing and how badly he played letting down his side, the team of Mum-'n'-Dad.

*The other night dear, as I lay sleeping,*
*I dreamt, I held you in my arms,*
*When I awoke dear, I was mistaken,*
*And I hung my head and cried.*

Wasn't all bad, because it was taken in good spirit and he was applauded for his efforts as he left the piano, even though he knew it was out of kindness – maybe pity? – for him, on their behalf.

Another vitally important point: a 'saving grace' moment, was the fact that this little episodic scene WASN'T witnessed by his mates, the boys-in-the-road, because if they'd been present to what transpired, he'd have been subject howls of delighted derision, followed by days-n'-days of painful ridicule.

He glanced quickly up toward the ceiling, roof and beyond that to the Heavens in a sigh of silent gratitude!

Shortly thereafter, Mum sought him out and asked if he'd had enough to eat and drink? When he assured her, pushing out his stomach and puffing out his cheeks with a grin, to emphasise as much, and to convince his mum, she whispered, not unkindly. "I think you ought to go upstairs to bed, now. You can take your comics up and a library book, and you can leave the light on. I'll pop up later to put your light out. Alright?"

That was okay by him and he took himself off, but not before collecting an empty plate and piling on another sandwich and a cup of milk; then took himself up the stairs to his bedroom.

Closing the door didn't really help in keeping out the sound, because the singing, laughter and commotion of the party going on downstairs carried under his door and into the room and interfered with his comic reading. He'd now changed into pj's, but did make an effort to concentrate on reading, but the raised levels of merriment below, despite his bedroom door being shut, still carried through.

The muffled, but loud voices and the conviviality, brought him off his bed, sneaking barefoot through the bedroom door to the head of the stairs, He began creeping stealthily down them to a halfway point, where he could easily peer through the banisters to watch the frolics and listen to the happy banter taking place, noticing also that the record player was back on, playing popular records of the latest releases.

He heard someone say in an inviting friendly voice. "Give us a song, Fred?"

His dad, with a half filled pint glass of beer, rose to the invitation and smilingly accepted.

He began, from a standing position in the centre of the room, turning to those around him.

> "How are things in Glocca Morra?
> Is that little brook still leaping there?
> Does it still run down to Donny cove?
> Through Killybegs, Killkerry and Kildare?"

He was in full voice and genuinely enjoying himself. Even his mum was smiling, because whatever entertainment qualities he lacked, he wasn't short of putting across a popular song in a strong singing voice.

Watching and grinning through the banisters, he admitted to himself that he and his brother didn't take after their dad. No singing voice or even the ability to get anywhere near an acceptable effort, but it was nice to hear his dad sing his heart out and all the more when at the end of it, he was warmly and spiritedly applauded.

He saw one of the American military policemen, lift a wrapped package from his overcoat pocket, which turned out to be a bottle of something-or-other?

"Here you go!" the military policeman said, flourishing the full bottle in the air above his head for all to see. "Genuine…" and here, the US serviceman read the label out loud, pronouncing it as 'cain-tuky bourbon', whilst his glimpse of the label read 'Kentucky Burbon'.

Partygoers filtered singly out of the front room to visit the lavatory outside the backdoor from the kitchen, and it was during one of these excursions that he was spotted by one of the American servicemen.

"What choo doin' up there?" the uniform laughed, standing still after catching sight of the pyjama-clad youngster, crouching on the stairs, staring down through the banisters. When Mum appeared, distracted by his comments, he made a move to return to his bedroom.

"Thought you'd gone to bed?" she teased.

"Here!" the American said, pulling a wrapped chocolate bar from his pocket and passing it up to him, through the banisters. "You like Candy, don't yuh?"

He nodded back with widened eyes.

The question was a no-brainer!

He reached out and clutched at the proffered gift, beaming, then scampered back up the remaining stairs and back to his bedroom. Just before doing so, he heard the American voices, saying.

"Yeah, let's make a little space in here. Got to have us some dancing room."

A woman's voice giggled. "Don't think we have room to walz?"

"Heck, no," came back cross-the-pond accent. "We gonna do some jitter-bugging, tonight!"

After that, the sounds from down-stairs sounded like a herd of buffaloes were running through their front room…

With the door closed once more, and sat cross-legged in the middle of his bed, he carefully examined his gift.

It was a chocolate bar, sure enough, and the wrapper read in print 'HERSHEY'S MILK CHOCOLATE'.

He turned it over in his fingers, carefully tore away the brown and silver paper, pulled the torn pieces back and away from the chocolate bar end, protruding. His head leaned forward and open-mouthed, gently bit off the scrumptious end chunk and chewed it, his taste-buds thoroughly enjoying the performance and experience.

"Beats chewing gum!" he told himself – and to the empty room, already taking yet another bite.

More joyful sounds of music and merriment flowed up from downstairs and into his bedroom, as the party got into high gear. He couldn't prevent himself from jumping out of bed, his inquisitiveness taking over, and once more to inching furtively along the darkened landing to the head of the stairs; then down a step-or-two, to stare in through the open doorway to the front room, where the assembled revellers, hand in hand, joined into an uneven circle to dance and the sing the Hokey Cokey:

*You put your left hand in,*
*Your left hand out,*
*In, out, in, out,*
*You shake it all about.*
*You do the hokey cokey,*
*And you turn around.*
*That's what it's all about!*

Followed by the chorus – and he grinned to himself with delight – 'cos he knew that right hand, left leg, and et cetera, would follow Great fun and exciting for him, huddled and sitting on the second stair down, to listen and watch, his eyes moving from one individual to another. They were getting around to lustily sing songs that even the tone-deaf would recognise and could sing to!

Best of all, Mum and Dad were in great form and thoroughly enjoying the evening, too!

**War News!**

- German Wehrmacht launches a winter offensive in the Ardennes forest against thinly positioned US units and force a break through with their intended goal a Belgium port of Allied supply debarkation, which had become a major supply point.
- US 101st Airborne Division is encircled at Bastogne by German Panzer Corps.

- As fog and low-cloud lift, Allied Air Forces swoop to attack enemy ground targets (vehicle and troop concentrations) in and around the Ardennes Bulge.
- British and US armoured units halt German Panzer Division seeking to break through Allied Lines toward the port of Antwerp
- Combined units of Marshall Tito's Yugoslav Partisans, Soviet 3rd Ukrainian Army and assisted by the Bulgarian Army, force a German retreat from Belgrade.
- British, American and Chinese Forces combine to launch fresh offensives against the Japanese in Burma, crossing the Irrawaddy River and advancing on Meiktila, at the centre of Japanese control in the region.
- German Forces in Greece surrender to Allies. Civil war breaks out between Communist and Royalist supporters but ends quickly after British military intervention and a subsequent truce.

## 23. A New Experience

His first parade was this coming Sunday. There was to be an inspection beforehand in the cellar of the church, after the eleven o'clock service, which was mandatory for members to attend.

On the day, and at the service, he noticed that the company first met in the cellar of the church before filing up and taking their seats together in the pews before the service commenced. There was a lot more hymn singing than at St John's, he compared. Also, less prayer rituals and chanting, but then he recalled that St John The Baptist was regarded as 'High Church', some saying that it was more like a Catholic mass, than a Protestant service?

This didn't occupy much of his thinking because he was only reluctantly attracted by the need to compare. He accepted, whatever? He was all geared up for the parade, and the march that followed, thereafter. The band would lead the marching company around the local streets where a few local people and kids, he had previously been told, would be attracted by the music of the band, would come out of their houses to watch. There was always a small crowd on the pavements as the company marched past, and most times the watchers would quietly applaud with their token of approval.

He'd taken some time at home in his bedroom, clean white shirt, dark tie with Windsor-knot and highly polished black shoes. Used the big mirror in his mum's bedroom, and worked at getting the right balance of his 'pill-box' uniform hat top gear in the right position that suited him, on his head and with a tidy quiff showing in front. However, come the inspection in the cellar, after the service and prior to stepping out onto the road adjacent, for the march that first Sunday morning, the captain took exception to his 'quiff'. The CO had stepped along the line of boys to order stockings pulled up to underneath the knee-cap, if they'd slid down, neckties adjusted and properly knotted, if otherwise. Then there was his quiff which attracted the captain's attention. Nothing, it would seem, escaped his notice in the dress inspection ritual. The CO's eyes stared firmly through his spectacles at the hair-out-of-place violation. His polished shiny baton came up and he poked the quiff loose-a'-floppy in expert manner, displaying it in an untidy mess.

"Remove your hat and comb your hair back, flat, lad; then replace it firmly and straight on the top of your head in the correct manner," he ordered curtly.

He nearly died of shame and felt the other boys must've been watching – smirking – and noting his discomfort. Later, he learned that this conclusion couldn't be further from the point because they were concentrating on their own appearance, and – shortcomings, perhaps – in passing muster?

Out on Richmond Park Road, the band at the head of the formed-up column, the rest of the company behind in three ranks preceded by their officers, with the captain taking up the rear position, together with a fellow officer.

The drum major raised his mace on high, and those behind, not only in the band, but in drawn up columns, became silent and aware, in readiness for the off.

From his position in the middle rank, and the new boy, he was able to take in and notice every movement ahead of him. The column waited as the mace rose into the air, then signalled – descending – the start of the march, a lone officer detaching himself from the head of the troop to take up position at the centre of the T-junction on Breck Road, and to hold up road traffic, temporarily, as the drum major – who, he was informed – provided the commands and leads the march, directed what the band had already rehearsed midweek, when to play, signalled the start with the side and kettle drums commencing the drum-beat roll.

The column turned left onto Breck Road and headed up toward the next junction, keeping well over to the left to allow other road users: cars, motor-bikes and cyclists, to overtake, without too much difficulty or delay. It crossed his mind, should a tram-car appear going either way, they might have to move even further over into the gutter at the side of the road in order to allow it to edge past. This situation didn't arise.

Now the bugles kicked in and blared their loud tones from the score of an army marching composition: '*The British Grenadiers*' that was followed by something sounding very much like 'You're in the Army Now!'

He more than enjoyed the excitement of marching in column with the other boys to the stirring strains, following the drum-an'-bugle band at the head, and leading. Concentrated most of the time on keeping in step with the brigadiers around him. He found himself lifted and he thought it was really great. Didn't march far, he guessed. Just a few streets up onto Belmont Road and back on an alternate route.

He enjoyed the first-time experience of marching ranks, so-much-so, he couldn't keep the smirk which engulfed his face, and must've looked – he guessed – like some half-wit who couldn't control his features, but he cared even less. This was something new for him, and he absorbed the thrill of a new belonging.

**War News!**

- US Army drives a wedge in German defences north of Echternach.
- Battle for Ramree Island, off Burmese coast, ends in victory for British/Allied Forces

## 24. "You're to Report to the Headmaster's Office!"

"The Headmaster wants to see you," whispered the class teacher, or retiree brought back to the profession as a result of the war, and the drain of current teachers from the profession into uniform.

He recoiled in shock. He wasn't aware of the old male teacher arriving, suddenly and stopping at his desk unseen. About the only time pupils were sent to Dixie's office, was because of misdemeanour or behavioural misconduct, or the like?

He lingered for a second or two to collect his thoughts. Wanted to ask 'why?', but that wouldn't have been right or in keeping, and besides, this teacher wouldn't be likely to divulge the purpose, even if he knew. Chances were, that he didn't, and cared even less!

Teacher had removed himself and returned to the front of the class, bethought himself, stopped and turned to check if his request been responded to, yet? An old man's vexed frown replaced the boredom on his countenance.

"Let's not keep the Headmaster waiting!" he cautioned, fuming at the lack of response, also as an admonishment, because of the boy's lack or inclination or tardiness – as he saw it – to move himself.

He stared back at the teacher.

"Yes, sir!" he answered, and eased himself up and out of his desk, and stood in compliance and reply.

In the hallway, he lingered from one foot to the other for a while, outside the Head's closed office door off the main corridor through the school. He experienced a bout of anxiety, because as much as he tried to fathom out the reason for the Head wanting to see him, it didn't bode well. Normally, the only time – far as he knew – anybody was sent for to the Head's office, they were in some way involved in truancy, a misdemeanour, vandalism of one sort or another, and perhaps class disruption? This called for the required severe ticking off or worse, like six-of-the-best on each open palm. It was known that Dixie had a reputation of being able to dish out and lay it on when it came to chastisement and punishment for misdeeds.

Anxious, because he had no clue as to why his presence was required, so he couldn't conjure up an excuse or defence for any in or out of, school irregularities? Maybe, that was the whole idea. Not to let or allow him to learn about what he was to be accused of, so he couldn't think up, dream or invent a set of lies in time to answer the questions put to him?

This notion made him all the more fidgety.

It was the 'not-knowing?', which was the worst part of this lack of information.

His imagination was working overtime, which didn't help.

He'd already tapped on the door, and more than a minute had passed without response.

Suddenly, the door opened quickly and abruptly, the Head poking his head out through the opening.

"Oh, right!" was all the Head said, pulling the door open wider.

Dixie beckoned him in, his face serious and the lips compressed and firm.

Inside the study, the Head closed the door and shuffled around the back of a very untidy desk, pointing to an empty chair at the front and facing the desk. At this signal, he edged in front of the vacant chair, but remained standing, awaiting authority to seat himself.

"Sit – sit down! Be with you in a minute," said the Head, flopping down on a large office arm chair. Dixie immediately adjusted his specs, fussing with loose sheets of printed papers on the desk, which were piled untidily high on one side, with thick and bulging files on the other, amid a pile of paperbacks, magazines and a tomb of a dictionary.

He watched the Head reach into his jacket pocket and produced a packet of cigarettes and instinctively started to offer the open packet across the desk, then quickly corrected and thought better of himself.

"Oh – no, of course not!" he laughed, briefly and embarrassingly. A match was struck against the side of the matchbox, which flared and was used to light the cigarette between his lips; then blew out a cloud of blue-grey smoke, before continuing to busy himself with a jumbled mound of paperwork, the cigarette wedged firmly between fingers of his right hand, seemingly to ignore the other person in the room.

"Right," the Head finally said, flashing a brief glance in his direction across the desk, which mightily relieved him greatly, because it was obvious that this invitation was clearly unconnected with anything remotely unpleasant.

"You," Dixie began, addressing a single sheet of printed paper held between both hands, which he had to poke around and seek to salvage from the top of an adjacent heap, but audibly addressed the top-class visitor across the desk.

"You were one of three boys I tutored in basic geometry some weeks back, weren't you?"

He coughed and nodded in the Head's direction.

"And, I had you doing special homework assignments in connection with it, too, I believe?"

The boy again nodded, whispering an almost inaudible "Yes, sir!"

"Well, the reason I've got you here, this morning, is because I received this communication from the Liverpool Education Committee in Sir Thomas Street. Because there's a grave shortage of teachers at the moment, they've taken the unprecedented steps of trying to resolve this problem by training up a special intake of students. They've written to most elementary schools in the city asking them to select one or more suitable applicants to take a special teachers' training entrance examination as part of the scheme. I decided I'd select you to represent the school. What d'you think?"

He swallowed, coughed and grunted an unintelligible reply, while his mind wrestled with the shock.

"Like to become a teacher?" And without waiting for an answer, continued. "Pay's well, and there's always promotion to consider, not forgetting a good pension at the end of it all…" here the Head paused to allow a chortling laugh to break from his throat. "That's if you live long enough!"

It was too much, all at once.

Not something he'd ever thought about.

He was flabbergasted.

Unable to even frame a reply.

Dixie let the printed sheet of the official letter slip through his fingers and settle on the desk. He looked up across at the boy, who was trying his best to contain the mind-boggling offer. He needed time to consider the proposal.

"Well, what d'you think?" the Head engaged him, smiling.

Before he could think of a reply – any reply, the Head concluded for him, taking his silence as a 'Yes'.

"Good!" Knew you'd be interested. Right, well, here's the letter you can take home to your parents, so they can be informed about what this is all about," he said passing the printed letter to him."

"Yes sir!" he finally managed.

"And you'll be expected to turn up for the one-day test exam, next Thursday at nine o'clock at Shiel Road Institute, as a first step. If you pass? – and, I think you're capable – they'll write to me, and – ah, we'll take it from there."

In the silence that followed, the Head gave him a kindly smile; then stood, signalling the meeting was at an end.

"Oh, and let me have that letter back tomorrow morning with your mum-n-dad's signatures on it, there's a good chap."

Outside and alone in the deserted hallway, he stood quite still staring down at the piece of paper in his hand, to recall the conversation and assess the impact.

He felt a little light-headed, giddy and momentarily stunned, unfolded the printed sheet and read the contents for himself, yet again. Tried to anticipate his parent's reaction to this offer and concluded they'd be supportive.

## War News!

- British Far East commander General Slim organises the over run of Japanese defences in Burma with the capture of Meiktila, leaving the road open for the advance on Rangoon
- Forward units of the US First Army capture the bridge at Remagen intact, which allows the crossing to be used by American armoured columns.
- USAAF commences heavy bombing of Japanese naval bases at Kobe and Kure.

## 25. Sadness at the Roadside

The winter weather deteriorated. The country, as a whole, experienced a nation-wide spread of rain, snow and severe gales. In fact, a week of frequent squally wind and gales so bad, that at one point the highest wind gust of more than 113 mph was recorded at one location. After which, the snow followed and there were deep drifts around the city, which was received with glee by most kids who fought very vigorous snowball fights at the slightest provocation. Artistic examples of snowmen sprang up temporarily at various locations, overnight.

The rest of the population were not impressed and regarded the widespread bad weather as a hindrance. Gangs of workmen were hurriedly called out onto the streets busiest thoroughfares to shovel and brush away the snow-n'-slush and spread large amounts of road-salt at all major junctions. It was especially required, because of the danger to shire horses used for dragging heavy loads to and from the docks area and slipping on iced-over slippery cobblestones, with the resultant danger and damage to life-n'-limb and not only the equine animals, but humans too.

He had occasion to take a letter from the Head into town to be delivered to the Liverpool Education Committee on Sir

Thomas Street. Dixie, explained he'd overlooked the deadline for the correspondence, and its contents were needed by head office.

He, the messenger, liked the idea, because he'd get away from class and there was always lots to see, going on, in town. In fact, there was a hold up on the dock road, while American mustang (P-51) fighter planes delivered and unloaded from merchant vessels, having arrived as a convoy from the US. They were being towed in a long straggly line, some minus wings, headed out toward Speke airport, where they'd be properly assembled and flown to where they were required.

After passing over the special 'hot' letter at reception in the Liverpool Education Office, he'd decided he wanted to look at the musical instruments behind the recently replaced windows of Rushworth & Dreaper's music shop, by the Old Haymarket on Commutation Row.

Ahead of him, a team of horses had been labouring up the hill on William Brown Street, pulling a particularly heavy load on a flat wagon and were finding their way more than difficult in the slippery conditions. The lead shire horse, a strong draught stallion with enormous pulling capacity, had suddenly slipped on the treacherous surface of the cobbles and gone down with a sickening crunch. The pulling load halted, immediately. The middle-aged carter, sat on his exposed position, immediately applied the handbrake and locked the wagon wheels, preventing it from slipping or sliding rearwards. His assistant, a younger man in his teens, sat stony-faced and watching.

The carter jumped down from his seat and hurried quickly forward and was immediately sickened, because he saw at once that the horse had severely damaged or broken one or maybe even both front fetlocks. The animal showed heartbreaking signs of distress.

He called out to a policeman in the vicinity, who was talking to someone in a stationary police radio car. The carter shouted for help and the policeman responded instantly with a waved arm.

The old carter ran back to the scene. He knew his horses like his own family, it was said. He looked across the road at the sad scene and saw that the old man was visibly upset as he knelt by the stricken animal, with tears starting to run down his cheeks.

To his young eyes, it was a shocking scene!

The horse, clearly in pain, was slumped forward and on its side, every now-and-again, trying to ease its pain and attempting to rise up, neighing loudly, it's head and neck thrashing in frightened terror. It's every movement only made things worse, but the wet-eyed carter clung to its neck, talking quietly to it.

The young assistant carter had now clambered down and stood at the kerbside speaking in hushed tones to two curious bystanders.

He inched forward toward them so he could eavesdrop.

Heard the young carter say. "Ernie, alwus – or most times, would sleep in the stables, when things went wrong."

"Went wrong?" one of the onlookers queried.

"Well, sometimes them big shire stallions would fight each other."

"Over what?" the astounded onlooker probed.

"Well," the young carter stumbled to explain. "They…sometimes, they'd he'd…the lead horse would get in a fight with a young stallion on account of one of the mares."

"Really?"

"Oh yeah! Big bust-up in the stables at night."

"You don't say?" the man managed, surprised at the thought.

The old carter was still on his knees with his arms about the huge horse's neck, talking gently and stroking its head, and trying his best to pacify it.

A dark van drew up quickly with a squeal of brakes at the kerb, some feet away from the accident. A man in a brown overall, stepped from the passenger seat carrying a small bag with the words 'veterinary' printed on the side of it, which he placed on the kerb. The man swiftly hurried back to the injured horse, where he stooped to look more closely and assess the damaged to the animal's forelegs and more closely at what some might call the fetlocks.

The carter was helped up onto his feet by the policeman and stood to one side, wiping away the tears from his cheeks and eyes.

The vet in the brown overall, continued to lean forward and seek the answers he was looking for.

Finally, he turned serious-faced to the carter and sadly shook his head, which caused the carter further great sadness and distress. He appeared to suddenly lose control and turned away to face the shop window, momentarily, to hide his sorrow.

A crowd had now collected on the pavement and spilled out into the road around the injured horse. The policeman decided, after a word with the vet tending the injured horse, to move the people back and away.

The vet spoke quietly to both carters, after which they unhitched some of the harness and reins that were attached to the lead horse. The remaining horses were then released from the wagon and led away to behind it.

The old carter returned to the injured horse, knelt down with both arms around its neck, the shiny brass and polished leather harness collar, still in place, and wept unashamedly.

The crowd was moved back along the pavement, but not before he saw the vet in brown, step back to the van and then return with folding screens under his arms, which he now placed around the pain-wracked squirming animal.

He was no longer able to see the fatally injured horse or the elderly carter kneeling and clasping the animal's head in his arms, but did see the vet return to his bag, open it, and retrieve what looked like a hand gun.

The policeman was joined by two more flat-capped policemen who had arrived in a radio-car.

"There's nothing more to see!" the policeman spoke sternly at the small crowd, physically pushing everybody firmly away and telling them gruffly to disperse.

## 26. Joining In

"How do I go about joining the junior gym team?" he asked a new and friendly face at the next BB meeting, now underway under the church, on a night in the following week of his enlistment.

"You good on a horse?" the lively youngster questioned back, after his stint at a table tennis game.

"Horse?" he pained, disappointed by the perplexing question he'd just been asked.

"Yeah? In the gym?"

"I – ah, don't ride. – Horses, that is," was his guarded reply.

"No, stupid. – A vaulting horse."

He shook his head.

"You never heard of a vaulting horse?" the kid laughed open-mouthed and showing his teeth, like a bloody horse, wide-eyed and incredulous.

"No," was his hushed reply, already embarrassed by his own admission.

"Well," the new friend said, "there's one way to find out?"

They were joined suddenly by two other boys tugging at the laughing kid's arms and urging him to come back to the table for another game.

Before he allowed the two boy's request, turned and said aloud. "Junior team's meeting tonight, down at the school, along Richmond Park." And as he was finally physically dragged away, shouted over their shoulders. "WALK DOWN, YERSELF, AN' FIND OUT!"

Which he did and recognised the low one-story school building he'd passed earlier, on his way and when going to the meeting under the church. He could hear the shrill yell of young voices and the thud and scuffle of pounding feet on wood flooring, which advertised kids enjoying themselves, long before he got to the building, echoing out through open windows.

Was soon bounding up the stone steps and through the unlocked swing doors at the entrance, and into a short hallway, which led into a wide-open space classroom, devoid of removable chairs and desks, now piled up and along both sides of the room, temporarily.

Occupying the open space, were about a dozen or so youngsters of his age, in sports gear – shorts and singlets, engaged in a game of tag and others helping to carry gym equipment into the room, from out of an adjacent store closet. Two older boys and a senior BB officer, he'd recognised from previous attendance, appeared to be in charge of proceedings.

"Brought your pumps and shorts with yuh?" he was asked.

When he explained that he'd come to join the junior sports team, he was told to go change, borrow a pair of gym shorts and check with the other lads to see if they had a spare pair of pumps in the storeroom that would fit, then come back and join the main group.

He was in luck with temporary gear until he could arrange something with his mum, for next time. Found the rest of the boys, who were being divided into two teams for a race between a straight line of chairs at opposite ends of the room.

"You might be just too old for the junior team?" he was told, when giving his details to the junior team coach, who added. "Supposed to be eleven or under. Still, join in for the moment. We're not competing against anybody serious, within the foreseeable future, only 'friendlies', so you'd probably pass."

He smiled back, happily, and nodded his thanks. It would've been a blow if he'd have been turned down, because participating in sports was what he was all about, when he didn't have his nose buried in a library-subscribed 'Biggles' novel.

"You any good?" the coach murmured to him, after he'd thought on and asked, as an afterthought.

"'Course!" he replied with a confident grin, knowing he could outrun anybody in his school class; could out swim any of them over the length at the baths – Lister Drive Baths that is.

"C'mon on, then," the coach ordered, turning to the other boys waiting to get started in a two-team relay race.

He was the last of four in his group, to race between chairs at opposite ends of the room, running from and returning to the start chair.

They were fast, he thought as the race began. His turn was rapidly coming up.

His chance to shine.

Because the other team's last man was off and ahead, seconds before he was, he had reason to fling himself forward, as his team's third man came in to the finish. Had to make up for lost time AND distance…

Heart going like a trip-hammer!

Feet-n'-legs digging in on the wood slats underfoot...

Arms pummelling back-n'-forth...

Could see the other team's number four was turning at the half-way return stage, as he caught up, braked, his borrowed pumps squeaking against the wood surface as he forced a sudden stop, bent his body to make the turn on himself, twisting and accelerating away on the final lap...

Immediately thrilled to find he'd shortened the distance...

Ran in a renewed burst of outpouring energy to catch the other lad.

Both crossed the finish line...

Together!

Too much cheering, back-slapping and noisy appreciation...

He knew, in his heart and despite his breathlessness, that he'd clinched his place in the team, and in their acceptance of him.

That was important, he knew.

He beamed with satisfaction.

After the dashing excitement of the relay race and allowing the boys to catch their breaths and get their second wind, the coach directed some of the boys to go fetch the vaulting horse and the other bits, from the store room.

They struggled out with it and he saw them set it down on all four adjustable legs in the centre of the room. Without needing further words, the boys scampered back into the store room and returned with the spring board and a large mattress being dragged along the floor, which were arranged front and back, the horse being set long-end on and ready for basic exercises.

"Okay," the coach clapped his hands together to shush the noisy chit-chat and call for silence and their attention.

"We're just doing basic exercise, here. Run up to the spring board, leap onto it raise and extend both arms up to the ceiling. Let's go through that first, so that you're comfortable with running onto the spring board to leap up on it; then step off the board and the next boy follows suit. C'mon, we' did this last week, so it shouldn't be new to you lot!"

Laughing and gurgling, the lads formed into a single line at the far end of the room, running forward one after the other to the spring board and jumping up from it with arms outstretched above their heads, until the last boy had completed, which was the new boy to the class.

"'Kay, now I want you to watch me as I run to the spring board, jump onto it and then leap up onto the horse itself. The pommels have been removed, so there's nothing to get in your way when you land on the top of the horse in the crouch position, hands on either side to steady yourself."

Coach ran easily up on the approach, stepped onto the board and then jumped in one movement up and onto the horse in the crouch position, before sliding off sideways and walking to one side.

"Now, don't worry about wobbling and falling off the horse, because me or one of my assistants will be on hand on both sides to catch you, if you slip. After the crouch position, stand up, walk to the end and drop off onto the mattress."

Everybody looked up their places, either in a single file awaiting the signal to start, and the coach plus his assistants moving both sides of the horse, and at the mattress to catch the boys dropping safely onto it.

Didn't all quite go to plan, because new boy mistimed his jump onto the spring board, with his momentum causing him to stumble forward off the spring board and cannoning into the end of the horse, knock him down, all the air out of his lungs and winding himself.

Coach leapt forward and helped him regain his feet.

"You okay?" he asked, somewhat concerned.

An embarrassed new boy, flushed, red-faced and aggrieved, but had to accept the giggling laughter from the rest if the boys, but in good taste. He smiled his acknowledgement back at them.

"Yep – okay," he managed.

"You done this, before?"

"No – er, no…"

"Don't worry. All new kids come to grief, first time. Go back an' do it again. Only, this time, concentrate on the jump at the spring board, to let your body get the feel of it – the reaction of jumping on it for the first time, 'kay?"

He nodded his head vigorously, to show his understanding.

Returned to the end of the room, and made his second run toward the horse, again.

No probs!

As he stepped off the board, before they prepared for the second part of the exercise, and the run-up to leap onto the horse…

To crouch…

To steady themselves, arms out wide…

To stand…

To drop off the back onto the safety mattress.

He managed all that, without mishap.

All good fun, he told himself and pleased with his efforts.

## 27. Politics Raises Its Head Above the Parapet

The talk amongst the kids in the road about the ongoing war, was mostly what they'd heard their parents say, listening in and eavesdropping adult conversation. There was talk of a coming general election, too. Although Winston Churchill, the prime minister, was expected by some to be re-elected, together with his Tory conservatives, it was no sure thing! There were those that said the men in the armed forces, and from the mass of lower-rankers, were determined to vote in a Labour government.

Leastways, politics was certainly not a subject high-up on kids' chit-chat, instead there was the usual blanket interest in what films were being shown, had been shown – and was about to be, at the local flea-pits?

Other subjects were about when the football fixtures lists would restart?

Who would be the next man up to challenge Joe Louis for the world heavy-weight boxing championship?

Was Jack Pye really the best wrestler at the Stadium on Bixteth Street in Liverpool?

It must've been about three weeks to a month, later, after he'd gone through the stress and strain of sitting a special teachers training exam at Shiel Road Institute, that he was summoned to the Headmaster's office.

When he'd entered the office, had – at the Head's signal – seated himself in the same chair across the desk from the big man, where he waited in hesitant silence while Headmaster re-read a letter he held in his left hand in front of him on the desk. A desk which still was an untidy mess, with papers, pamphlets, magazines and books scattered willy-nilly.

"They've written to me about the results of that special teacher training examination, you and many others especially selected from schools across the city, took some weeks ago."

"Yes sir," he managed respectfully, staring hard at the back of the letter, and over it at the Head's expression behind those specs of his, trying to read something into it, and failing in the effort.

"They," the Head began again.

In his mind the word 'They' loomed large, but as headmaster had not divulged who 'They' were, he assumed he must mean the Liverpool Education Committee?

"They," the Head started again, "have revealed that there was only a limited number of vacancies to fill, which was less than the total number of boys selected and sent for this – ah, initial screening."

Another pause, while the boy's intent eyes stared across the other side of the desk and attempted or sought to read the headmaster's mind.

Again, without success.

Mr Dixon abruptly looked up from the correspondence and over and directly into the boy's face and those young eyes filled with expectation.

The Head relaxed and compressed his lips, displaying a kindly disposition.

"You didn't quite make it, my boy, but," and here, he raised those bushy eyebrows of his and squinted beneath them once more at the letter before him.

"You – you, did very well, but," and his face expressed a grimace before continuing.

"You didn't do well enough."

The recipient of his information experienced mixed emotions but gave away no sign of inner emotion or of how he'd received the news, presenting a wooden inscrutable expression.

"Did well, lad. Didn't embarrass the school or yourself in the effort, but – I s'pose – it just wasn't your day," the Head finished speaking. He signed, expressively, looked up again, grinned and began to rise up from his chair.

"However, there'll be other opportunities, along the way. Make sure you parents – your dad, and so forth, know about the contents of this communication. The result, that is."

"Yes, sir," he replied, observing the signal by way of physical movement, that the brief appointment was ended.

The Head extended his hand to the boy's surprise, and he tentatively responded.

Outside, on the corridor, a moment of reflection. Was he really that close to passing the initial stage? Or was it, p'raps, the Head speaking kindly, choosing his words, to save him from too much inner disappointment, torment and embarrassment, and possibly feeling bad about it?

As he was not shown the letter, explaining his failure, there was no way of knowing?

On the return, and during his solitary walk back to class, he had puzzling feelings of relief.

P'raps, it wasn't to be, he told himself?

Upon reflection he be-thought, dismissively, didn't want to teach a bunch of snivelling snotty-nosed kids, anyway!

- German Forces launch second offensive against thinly spread US army positions south of the Ardennes as part of the Wehrmacht's Operation Nordwind, and in the area of Colmar, Alsace-Lorrain, France. Earlier German offensive aimed at Antwerp necessitated siphoning off of US units urgently needed to reinforce and bolster Allied countermoves to halt this previous advance.
- British troops mount amphibious landings on Akyab Island, as part of Operation Talon against Japanese army occupying emplacement and locations in Burma.
- German civilians flee East Prussia in the face of further Russian Army onslaughts and penetration of Wehrmacht defences in the region, as part of the Soviet push toward the vistula. Refugees clog roads leading to the battlefront and hinder German reinforcements.
- British naval units involved in attacks against German convoys departing Norwegian waters and headed to the Baltic Sea. Later, German Kriegsmarine Narvik-class destroyers recalled from Tromso, Norway, were also attacked returning to German home waters.

- Fourth inauguration of Franklin D. Roosevelt, after recent elections in America, at the White House (normally held in the US capital, Washington), vice president Harry S. Truman is sworn in, also.

## 28. Sound of Music Attracts

He was present, having come early this particular evening to the 23$^{rd}$ BB evening in the cellar of Holy Trinity church. Having just arrived, reporting in for instruction, as part of a course he'd applied for on semaphore signalling. The end goal was, to start with, the BB signaller's certificate (semaphore), which meant that with the next certificate for Morse signalling, he was entitled to enter for the BB Signaller's Badge. To him, this was worth aiming for: ability and recognition.

Semaphore signalling with flags, he learned, was used in the early eighteen-hundreds and especially between sailing ships. Although, he'd heard it said, the French had originally invented the system during the time of Napoleon, because of the problems of army communication.

He liked and took to the idea of being, in his vivid imagination, aboard HMS Victory, when Admiral Nelson sent his famous message to the captains of his fleet, before the Battle of Trafalgar, back in 1805: 'England expects every man will do his duty!' After which, Horatio led his ships to destroy or capture fifteen French and Spanish ships-of-the-line for nil losses to the British fleet.

So, it wasn't hard for him to practice for the semaphore flag course, with his wild mental imagery working overtime, him clambering up and onto the crosstrees of HMS Victory, the wind and sea-spray in his hair, flagging forth his hero's message to the fleet before commencement of battle.

How stirring can that be?

He also, couldn't fail to notice that evening, that the band members had also assembled in the main cellar for band practice. However, he'd never heard – been up close in a confined space – when they were at practice. So, when they struck up the first chords of a march, he was shocked rigid by the shattered silence and instantaneous thunderclap of bugles and drums. The march to be played at next Sunday's parade. This detonation of noise, which combined the shrill of bugle blasts and rapid beat of percussion, he found ear-splitting, but thrilling at one and the same time.

In the side room, where the semaphore class was held, a classmate laughed out loud. "You should see your face!" he exclaimed.

He turned back from the open door and joined in his risibility.

"Wow-ee!" was all he said.

Classmate added. "We're finishing up, now. This is why we began the semaphore class early, before the band practice 'cause you can't hear yerself think – never mind, talk!"

"Yeah!" he nodded. "See what you mean."

"The…" said the lad, the words obliterated and drowned out by the band recommencing practice.

"WHAT?" He shouted, grinning, fingers in both ears.

The lad just shook his head, and mouthed the word 'See yuh!' before taking his leave and removing himself through the doorway with the rest of the class and a wave of the hand.

He collected his scribbled notes and pencil, to follow them. He stepped through the door, but instead of walking along the wall past the band, to the exit, instead hovered a while, to watch and listen.

The music was loud and reverberated off the walls and ceiling. No matter, he liked the energetic sound and the emotion it generated. He could see and read the enjoyment reflected on the band members faces, some of whom were serious and staring to the front, whilst others concentrated on their contribution, still others – the drummers, some of whom had their eyes fastened on the conductor and especially his wielded baton in air.

Fascinated and still smiling his pleasure, he continued to idle against the wall.

The synchronisation was not quite right and the bandmaster flourished his baton testily, bringing proceedings to an abrupt halt, some bugles blasting a half-a-note spiralling shriek, together with the odd drumstick, tapping down, unprepared.

"Right, boys," their conductor said, "let's start again from the beginning, and get it together, this time!"

The leader raised his baton, while the whole band readied themselves.

For the first time, he took note of the bandmaster: about six-foot tall, give-or-take a little, middle-aged, ruddy complexion, small trimmed white moustache, clear widened blue eyes that missed nothing, he guessed. Topped by a fine mane of grey hair, swept firmly back. He wore a smartly pressed dark suit, below which a pair of highly polished black shoes poked out under the lower end of his pant-legs. The finished article, he thought. A band conductor as opposed to a symphony orchestral leader, he'd seen at the pictures, once, with a bounce of unruly long hair, which he shook about. In fact, his whole being pranced and gyrated to the musical movement.

Different band, different orchestra.

Why the difference in dress appearance and motion?

Suddenly realised he was alone on the side wall, watching and listening, so moved himself toward the exit, but didn't want to leave just yet.

This time, the piece of march music the band played, must've been to the bandmaster's satisfaction, because he didn't interrupt, whilst it was played. At the conclusion, he told the boys to relax and take a breather. There was an immediate hum of conversation, the placing of instruments on nearby tables or even the floor, as the ranks opened and the members fussed around in groups or couples.

Two members, close to him, began turning the screws on the side of their drums to tighten the skin, which attracted his attention and he inched-up on them to watch. Both boys became aware of his solitary presence and looked up, questioningly?

By way of quick explanation, he said, "Just wondering why you were doing that?"

"Didn't sound right," one tousled fair-haired lad replied.

He just nodded his understanding, but he hadn't really understood.

The two carried on chatting, and he should've moved away out of range and out of politeness, but he didn't, because he wanted to talk to them about the band and risked being accused of snooping or nosiness.

They paused in their chit-chat and both turned their heads in his direction?

"I…ah, just interested in what you're interest in?" and hastily added, because of how that must've sounded, "About the band practice – and all that?"

"Why? You wanna join the band?"

"Well…" he said awkwardly, not wanting to be too forward.

"Bandmaster's looking' for new members."

"Really?" he sparked up, his face all aglow in reply.

Both kids nodded together. "We'll take you over to see him, 'kay?"

After a 'Come early, next week, and see me' from the officer in charge of the band, he almost danced and skipped his way home.

## 29. Adolescent Itinerant

A school break occurred toward the end of the cold rainy, sleeting, winter season, and the start of spring. Wasn't really the weather that suited outdoor pursuits. Kick about in the road wasn't always on. They'd – the September Road boys, and him – would sometimes set off for the nearby park to participate in a game of football or to just run around the perimeter to keep fit. No fun, when the 'heavens opened', and they were caught out in drenching rain.

In fact, as he thought about it, he noticed it was just starting to rain, yet again.

Couldn't always rely on his mates being available to play out or to call on, for indoor chats. So, it was a case of looking elsewhere to fill the boredom. Standing inside the front room window, staring out through heavy slanting drops of rain on the outside window and thrown against it by gusty winds, and beyond it an empty road, does absolutely nothing to foster enthusiasm in anything!

He shook his head and frowned.

Mum and Dad were at work at that time on a weekday morning, being about nine o'clock, or the normal time he'd be at school.

The house was empty.

He'd read his latest Biggles book from the local library.

He wrestled with the thought of going into town and just drifting around in and out of shops, but that wasn't such a great idea, because he didn't like visiting department stores with clothing and house wares on display and for sale.

A right bore!

Besides, it would still be raining, he knew, in town.

Back in his bedroom, he checked out his moneybox and loose change in the top drawer of his chest-of-drawers, foraging through the mass of rubbish he couldn't seem to part with but was pleasantly surprised to discover he was better off financially than he thought.

The No. 29 tram conveyed him into the city centre and finally dropped him off near the corner of Commutation Row and Islington, just before eleven o'clock. Wasn't far from the spot where the shire horse had fallen heavily, broke both front fetlocks and had to be 'put to sleep', as they called it.

The late morning traffic of trams, buses, lorries, vans, horse-drawn carts, and the odd motor car were in stop-start mode, and the pavements were busy with people scurrying by and going about their business, queuing up for this-n'-that – and the other? There was a mentality amongst adults – or so it seemed to be, to him – that whenever they – grownups – saw a queue, they'd join it, before even finding out whatever it was they were queuing for? He regarded this attitude as crazy crack-pot goings-on, but then he was only a local snotty-nosed school-kid, and what did he know about why old-enough-to-know-better, persons, queued?

He walked past the Empire Theatre. Thought he saw a blow-up picture of the singer and 'Forces Favourite' – as she was commonly referred to – Vera Lynn, on the billboards outside, singing with a 'Big Variety Company'. All the rage during these war years, were these well-supported musical events, which seemed to be ENSA presentations going around the country's theatres and the world, entertaining the troops and civilians, alike. The last of the panto, Cinderella, was still playing, he noted.

He mounted the steps into Lime Street railway station and walked off to where the train-schedule board was lit up and a knot of people were stood looking up and reading the train times. He stared at the trains drawn up on the platforms. One had a 'Manchester' sign on it.

He paused, and suddenly had a brain-wave. The urge to take the train to Liverpool's closest city, which was only about thirty miles or so away was pretty strong and took him over by storm. Explore pastures new, yeah?

Kid's Day Return?

How about that, he asked himself, silently?

The train clattered out of the station with his face almost pressed against one of its grimy un-washed windows in the carriage, his return ticket folded carefully away and thrust deep into a trouser pocket.

Couldn't, mustn't, lose it, he told himself.

This was the first time he'd travelled ALONE on a train, which was new experience and gave him a sense of awareness, maturity and purpose, he hadn't felt before.

He'd never done this, ever. going off somewhere on his lonesome, without first discussing it with Mum and Dad. He grimaced momentarily at the thought of how Mum would've reacted, had he consulted her, first.

But yes, it was a great feeling.

Exultation!

Freedom!

Mischievous, – reckless? And yes – a tad naughty!

It was only to Manchester, and then the return ride back to Liverpool, he idled in thought.

What did he know about Manchester?

Big city in the northwest...

And?

...Next question?

He looked around and was aware that the carriage compartment was not completely full. Glanced sideways at a middle-aged woman trying, very badly, to control two six-year-old boys; three soldiers in uniform playing a card game; two nuns wearing those enormous white headgear, which looked for all the world like mini sails; two foreigners wearing odd clothes and speaking rapidly to each other in loud whispers, in an alien tongue.

Spies?

A young woman in specs reading a paperback, which judging by the cover illustration was a murder thriller or mystery? An airman in RAF blues, with a 'Canada' patch sewn onto his shoulder. What part of Canada, he pondered? Didn't know much about the country, 'cepting that had a western concept, the Calgary Stampede.

Turning back to the window, he saw that the train was now rushing through countryside: trees, shrubs, the odd farm houses-n'-barns, cattle in isolated fields all whizzing past. Reminded him of when he was evacuated some years back, to Warton, staying at Green Gates with his Auntie Nelly, but that was another story...

Although the train occasionally stopped at odd stations, it wasn't until they all started to move themselves, that he was immediately aware most of the passengers in his carriage, were making preparations to alight at the next station, collecting newspapers, bags, raincoats and other miscellaneous items. Maybe, Manchester? The train was rapidly losing speed and braking and he was aware of the reduced speed, and his need to be in readiness for stopping at the next station on the line, which had to be Piccadilly, Manchester, he guessed, listening to the muffled utterances around him.

He was right. Quickly jumped up to join other passengers alighting onto the noisy platform. Noisy, because the station's PA system was blaring out information that sounded very much to him like a foreign language, and made as much sense?

He filed through the ticket barriers and out onto the station concourse, the exit and onto the open pavement and busy road running by.

Fairly open-minded about where to drift off to, and also knowing that it was just after midday, which told him the journey had been quicker and shorter than he'd anticipated, taking only three-quarters of an hour, he judged.

The very next thought was his belly. Was comforted by the bulge in his raincoat pocket, which he patted, further pleased in the knowledge that his sarnie-making powers had secured a culinary delight in the form of a cheese sandwich with plenty of margarine applied heavily smeared onto two thick slices of Devonshire tinned bread, with as much Cheshire cheese as he could pile in between. His mouth watered, temporarily, at the thought and he licked his lips in anticipation, but not yet the time to devour his meagre ration. After all, he wasn't – and didn't feel like – he was about to collapse from malnutrition, not yet. His brilliant forethought

– the tasty sandwich – he applauded himself on, had saved him from unnecessary outlay it would've cost to purchase the same in a local cafe.

Coming toward him and pulling to a stop at a nearby pavement bus stop, was a red and yellow (cream?) paint-sprayed Manchester Corporation double-decker bus. He was suddenly attracted to it and his eyes focussed. Not just an ordinary bus, but one with the name of a great destination – or, one of its destinations – in big letters above the driver's position: Belle Vue Zoo.

A cheerful conductress was very attentive to his enquiry and the fare. Wasn't too long before she informed him that his stop was coming up, next. After he'd stepped off the platform onto the adjacent pavement, she kindly pointed in the direction he had enquired about before bus drop off.

Wasn't too long, after stepping out, before he arrived outside the entrance to Belle Vue Pleasure Gardens and its Zoo. Across the road, opposite, he noticed Longsight railway station. P'raps, he thought, he should've taken the train?

Inside this exciting venue, there was just so much – too much to see, before he regretfully he had to depart, worried that he might miss connections and arrive home late. His sarnie well devoured and digested, by now.

He caught the bus going back into town with the same conductress aboard and they chatted about what he'd seen, before taking his leave at the railway station and catching the next train back to Liverpool.

Mum was already home from work, when he arrived back at the house, and he was fairly bubbling over with the story of his tourist trip-come-safari, short globetrotting train-n'-bus journey to a distant fields, full of liberating experiences and eye-opening search, and – simply put – pursuit of something new and different.

Such is the curiosity of the young at the start to their adolescence years!

Initially, shocked and concerned by his unusual action and not a little perturbed, Mum was absorbed by his telling of the day's adventure.

And yes, he told her, there were different types of animals in cages, but some were empty. Belle Vue is, he informed her, the third largest zoo in the country, so he'd been told. Had a lioness called 'Beauty', but the animals were affected by the shortage of food. For instance, he'd discovered there were no sea lions or penguins because they could only eat fish, and there just wasn't any in the amount that was required to keep them alive.

Whether she agreed with his out-of-the-ordinary trip or not, he wasn't sure. He didn't ask. Didn't put that awkward question to the test in case she disapproved of his solitary exploratory expedition and would put paid to any future idea by forbidding it.

He hoped she'd regard it as a one-off.

# 30. 'Into Each Life, some Rain Must Fall' – Really?

He had managed to get into the band. Not only that, but he was allowed to take the drumsticks home with him in order to practice the five-n'-seven-beat drum roll exercises on any hard surface, like a table.

Mum, who first doubted his claim to be a member of the band, was now convinced by the sight of the drumsticks in situ and was pleased for him, she said, even though his rattling and continuous practising nearly drove her mad.

The piano lessons saga was now history, he was relieved to understand. Mum didn't bring up the subject and he certainly didn't mention it. He was tinged with regret over letting her down, because she'd harboured expectant hopes in that direction. Didn't voice that opinion but must've thought so. She'd sometimes relive her youth and her early piano lessons. She possibly hoped, but didn't say, that he might have achieved some level of competency in that musical direction.

His pleasure at being accepted as a side-drummer was formally confirmed when he was selected, after many training sessions, which included the experience of carrying the side drum attached to his belt during early sessions under the church. He had now become an accepted member to march with the band and looked forward to the day when he'd make his first march through the streets.

This proud and momentous day took place at their next Sunday parade, out-n'-about, up-n'-down roads and streets in the neighbourhood. He thoroughly enjoyed the exercise and new found experience, even though he was initially a nervous wreck on his first parade. However, with the first effort over and another parade attended, as the new boy-in-the-group, full-fledged member of the band, his confidence knew no bounds and flowed freely. After just six weeks or so, he regarded himself as a veteran. Even allowed to take his side-drum home to clean and polish it.

For good reason: the Twenty-Third Company had been selected as the lead company in the annual Liverpool City march-past of BB companies, past St George's Hall on the coming Sunday of the month. This dominated their conversation and there was much anticipation and excitement enjoyed by the whole band, and the rest of the company, too.

It was, indeed, an honour for the 23$^{rd}$ Company of Boys' Brigade to lead the procession of companies past the saluting base.

No ifs or buts – just wonderful!

Came the Big Day of the BB Liverpool Companies march past at St George's Hall and the whole band and the rest of the company was there fidgeting, lined up on St John's Lane, next to St George's Gardens in their best uniform, bib-n'-tuckers', shoes polished bright-n'-shiny to a high gloss, stockings pulled up to beneath the knee-caps, hair cut short and flattened back with brylcream or vaseline hair tonic, drum screws, bugles, belt buckles and '23$^{rd}$' pill-box hat badges, shined and polished to excellence.

The Company was at ease, ready and awaiting the order to move.

For a change, he sighed in relief, it wasn't raining.

How about that?

Thank you, God!

There was a great deal of annoying waiting about, with questions as to why? left unanswered, which didn't do anything to ease the nervous tension, building.

All of a sudden, there was a shout of raised official voices followed by an immediate silence which descended on the ranks as conversations were cut, most halfway through, with bated breath and heightened listening in respect of orders about to be given and a readiness to jump-to-it, in response.

The lead company of the march past, $23^{rd}$ Company of Holy Trinity Church, Breck Road, were at the head of a long line of other companies, behind them, and at the junction of St John's Lane, alongside the huge and imposing edifice of St George's Hall, leading up onto Lime Street.

There was another long pause and then the lead Bandmaster of the $23^{rd}$, received a signal and called the band to attention, awaiting the final alert to march.

It came, and a thrill of excitement spread through the ranks, as – bearing up – some unable to conceal or prevent beams of delight showing on their scrubbed and shiny faces, the band stepped forward in perfect marching formation to the junction at Lime Street.

Following the Bandmaster's signal, with his raised mace, they wheeled left in formation up onto Lime Street, with the crowds lining the street to watch the ceremony. The massed onlookers on pavements, either side, broke into hesitant and broken applause, as they witnessed the well-rehearsed and strutting approach toward the saluting base; then halting.

The thin mace rose yet again and on signal to commence playing, the order to march was given, the bugles and drums sounding off together in rousing unison.

His position was front row centre, the side-drummer of the leading three, and he had his eyes fixed on the breeze-shifting black silk tassels at the back of the Bandmaster's black Glengarry, which was sat squarely on his head ahead of him.

The shrill screech of bugles and the rhythmic drumbeat roll and tattoo of side, kettle and base drums in unison, caused a wave of further excitement to ripple through the thronging crowds, pressed forward on the pavements on both pavements.

Their colourful presentation and military bearing in the approach along the centre of Lime Street, energised the applause and cheering, which rang out on both sides of the thoroughfare, from delighted spectators and onlookers, some of the relatives of those in the march and the rest attracted through press advertising ahead of the parade.

Several uniformed Liverpool City policemen were stationed at various intervals, stood in the gutters, along the crowd-lined route, to hold the crowd in respectful control at the edge of the pavements.

As the marching columns reached the Saluting Base, which included the prominence and majesty of His Grace, the Lord Mayor of Liverpool, the order was given.

"I-EYES, LEFT!"

And, as they passed, the band playing well and in masterly togetherness, proudly and enthusiastically, striking out in their musical delivery, the crowds, waved, pressed forward and shouted their 'Hurrahs' and cheered all the louder.

It was, indeed, it caused a heart-warming and electric response among the boys at the vanguard of the column and especially the members of the 23$^{rd}$ Company band.

An exultant euphoric tide flushed through his being, just a moment before – disaster struck!

His hands, wrists and arm movements were almost robotic in time to the music and united with fellow drummers, merging in a blur of practised and drilled uniformity.

That was until…

"I-EYES, FRONT" was heard as the lead column passed the saluting base.

And then…

Something terribly wrong!

Two drumsticks in his hands…

and the stick in one hand fluttered uncontrollably…

Instantaneously…

Shockingly…

Was no longer firmly held…

Horrifically, he'd lost a drumstick!

His wide, almost pop-out eyes, stabbed down…

What?

Where?

Why?

No time for this, 'cepting to keep on marching in step.

Continuing to use his left drumstick…

Aghast and conscious of smiling sympathetic faces in the crowd, pointing…

An emotional rush of humiliating shame and of apparent incompetence!

The column passed by the Empire Theatre frontage, and continued past the entrance to The Legs of Man public house, before wheeling right, following the direction of the mace-bearer, out of Lime Street and starting up London Road, with the men's tailors, Montague Burton's store, on their left, the crowds stationed there, seeing for the first time, the middle drummer in the front rank of the leading band, playing with only ONE STICK?

Quick recap told him he'd had felt just the slightest slip and finger twinge as the feeling of the drumstick in his right hand faded...

Hardly anything definite.

No real reason to glance down!

Just an immediate – strangeness?

By the time he knew it was...gone and had snatched a head-down snap check.

Too late!

Didn't step on anything on the road surface?

The urge to halt, turn around, was a NO-NO.

The inner stab and realisation of a blunder – HIS, was straining and very painful.

Funny thing – funny? – drummers on either side of him hadn't noticed, because they continued their rat-a-tat oblivious or ignored whatever, and maybe dismissed his plight?

Continuing to strum his left drumstick and even activate his empty right hand, raised up and down to face height, as required, seemed ludicrous, but the right thing to do?

Ahead in thought, he was stung by the expected and anticipated reaction to his incident.

When Bandmaster finally learned, when back at Holy Trinity church, what had occurred in his rear, he'd dismiss him from the band...for sure!

When word got around in the band and the rest of the Company...smirks and ridicule!

This must be the worst humiliation of his entire life!

His mouth was dry and his tongue lolled big and uncomfortable, trying to swallow.

Mum? – Mum would immediately tell by his face that something untoward had occurred...

Several hundred humiliating yards further on, abreast of T.J. Hughes department store, he received a painful prod in the small of his back. Instinctively, he half turned, but before he could perform a full twist, a drumstick was thrust firmly and roughly through his upper right armpit, delivered from behind by the boy in step immediately to his rear.

His whole being stiffened in instant relief and a wave of gratitude swept over him.

Rat-a-tat-tat, went both his drumsticks to beat in regular uniformity and consistency with fellow side drummers.

Solace. – A crumb of comfort, getting his drumstick back, while still on the march?

All was not lost!

## War News!

- Soviet army group enters Warsaw, as the Wehrmacht retreats to new defensive lines.
- RAF continues to pound targets in the Ruhr and Berlin, night-bombing in mass bomber formations. New target included Dresden.
- US Marines storm ashore on the Japanese-defended island of Iwo Jima.
- Russian armies converge to race into East Germany towards the stoutly defended German capital of Berlin.
- USAAF launches further air raids on the ball-bearing factories at Schweinfurt but suffer losses from Luftwaffe and ground flak defences.

# 31. Royalty and the Duke of York

"Did you know the King and Queen were in Liverpool?" one of the kids hanging around at the top of the road addressed his other peers of four, leaning up against the wall of the pub, bored, as usual.

This was one of the other places where the September Road boys usually congregated or hung out, after school, and while their evening meal was in the process of preparation for when they were expected back in the house, at about five-ish.

It was where they knew they'd find each other at the end of the day, and where they would raise or bring up topics from snippets of info they'd gleaned from their classmates, during their boring day at school, or from closer, at home.

As nobody had answered him, the lad who'd posed the question, tried again.

"Are yous deaf?" he repeated, but a little louder, this time.

"What's your problem?" one asked, looking up from his week-old comic, he'd dragged out of his bulging pocket, forcing it to be creased, from folded flat and dog-eared from constant movement, as well as being torn at the edges. He had to use some effort to drag it past the catapult he had stashed there, together with a balled-up snot-rag, which had once been what is called in polite society, a hand-ker-chief!

"No problem, jus' educatin' you lot about a Royal occasion," he glared back, annoyed because his item of info had been disregarded and he'd expected a big wide-eyed inquisitive, speculative overactive nosiness, not a damp-squib non-responsive negativity.

"You've upset him!" said would-be pianist, quietly observing from the side of group, sotto voiced.

"The lot of yous, not just him!" snapped their accuser, stung by the cynicism.

"Okay, so wadda yous want to say?"

Now, he had all their attention, and they waited to hear the spectacular news, evidenced by their presented facial appearances and – let it be said – undying attention. Only, the thing was, they'd missed or forgotten what it was he'd originally asked them?

In the silence, he stared angrily at their now questioning and innocent stares.

"Aw, forget it!" he said, swiping an imaginary wasp in the air in front of him and turning away to show his back and disgust.

"Ay, don't be that way!" argued one.

"Sorry, you're upset," grunted another, holding back a snort of laughter.

"Shit! That's the last thing you wankers are!" His head snapped back to verbally launch at them, wild-eyed.

"You wanted our attention, and now you've got it. WHAT?" remarked another voice.

"C'mon, don't be that way…"

"Hey, we're listenin'…"

Finally, a soothing voice uttered, "We're all palsy-walsy's, ain't we?"

There was a pause as they eyed his back, glancing furtively at each other and exchanging silent grins and deceitful winks.

After this show of apologetic contrition, the angry one turned back to face them.

"The King and Queen were here in Liverpool, today."

"Nothin' about them comin' up here to visit, in last night's Liverpool Echo?"

Angry one sniped back, "Well, there wouldn't be, twit-head! An' don't ask me why, 'cause you know WHY? Jerries would send over one of their top assassins to shoot dem, that's why!"

"How d'you know all this?" asked another.

"My dad seen 'em today down on the docks where he works."

"About assassinatin' dem?"

The informant ignored the question.

"What," asked another, "wus they doin' down there?"

"Signin' on for work," chortled another.

By now, the gang were all ears and eager to hear more.

"On board and visitin' a battleship in the Gladstone dock."

"Didn't know there was a battleship at the docks?"

Piano-player cautioned, in mock seriousness. "There's a war on, didn't you know?"

"And," their informative continued, "a newey, as well. Only launched in 1940."

"How d'you know that?" catapult owner, demanded.

"Me dad told me."

"Was it built at Cammell Lairds?"

"No. He said it was Glasgow."

"Sank the Scharnhorst with her fourteen-inch shells," added the pianist.

"No kiddin'," gasped the questioner, learning something, he didn't know, but in a better mood now that he'd definitely got their attention.

The speaker who'd revealed her armament, then asked. "So why was she here in Liverpool?"

Informant replied, in a hushed voice, conspiratorially. "Being reserviced," and volunteered. "Goin' out to the Pacific to join the Americans fightin' the Japs."

There were inhales of breath and a reassessment of the intelligence they just been handed.

"Did your dad see what they were doing to her, while she was in dock?" a bright spark, chipped in.

"Addin' all kinds of ack-ack guns, 'cause them Japs are using kamikazes."

"What's kami ka-kazees?", ventured a voice, unsure of the word or its pronunciation.

"Jap pilots crash their planes straight onto the Yankee warships…" he added.

"Instead of jus' using a bomb?"

"NO! With the bomb…with the whole thing…the plane, the bomb – every think!"

"What about the pilot?" another squeaked up, unbelieving.

"Him, as well."

"Wow!"

"Our fellahs, don't do that," squeaky said.

"Well," the Docker's son pursed his lips together. "That's what me dad said after talkin' to them sailors, on board."

"Your dad seems to know an awful lot?" spoke up a doubting-Thomas.

The boy shrugged his thin, bony shoulders. "If you don't believe me...?"

There was a thinking silence, while the huddled listeners, with big ears and inquisitive faces, digested all this riveting stuff.

"I saw the King and Queen, once," the piano player added, quietly, breaking into the conversation.

"When, – just now?" a voice asked, surprise laced into the question.

"No," he countered, "before the war, it was. – 'bout two years before the war."

"Where was that, then?"

"They were visiting Liverpool and my mum heard that they'd be visiting the Grand National. She must've been told the route they'd take to the course, because my dad was working back in Seaforth where we lived at that time, me mum – with some of her friends – took me to Queen's Drive, by the Mertons Pub. She sat me up on a sandstone wall, so I could see above the heads of crowds lining the road, when the cars came through carrying the Royal family. I was able to see them drive past and we all cheered."

There was a further moment of reflective silence after disclosure of this little anecdote; then smiles all around, because today had proved to be a very informative little get together for some of the September Road boys and proved not to be a bore. With plenty they could tell and talk about at the dinner table that night, they looked forward to meeting up with their respective families. Would be the centre of attention – for maybe a minute or so – instead of being dismissed as an irrelevance and told to be quiet, on account of their age, as was usually the case.

# 32. Liverpool's 'Coney Island' Part One

"We should go over to New Brighton," he suggested, stood out on the pavement in the warm morning sunshine with some of the September Road-ites. His mates, doing nothing important or interesting, just chatting generally.

It was called: gabbing.

"I think that's a good idea," a voice, further along the pavement, confirmed; then added, as an afterthought. "Wadda we do for dosh?"

"Just the tram and ferry fare," he answered, having already thought about it and guessed in advance that would be the first question following his suggestion.

"Then what?" another voice commented. "We wus there not long ago, at the open-air baths!"

He coughed a short dismissive. "All kinds…We could look in at the fun fair, go on the beach. All kinds of things."

"Why?" chipped in a tired voice.

"Why? Well, 'cause it's our own Coney Island, that's why."

"Coney Island?"

"That's what I've heard some grown-ups, call it. Like the one in New York, 'cepting that Coney Island isn't an island, but part of the mainland, with amusements, bright lights, an all that – same as New Brighton."

"So why compare?"

"It's our merchant seamen, who go there time-n'-time again. New York, that is. Because it has a fun fair and a beach, yeah?"

"So why call it Ler-pool's Coney Island?"

He shrugged his reply.

"Okay, it's not called that in the geography books or shown on the maps I've looked at. All the same, its local gossip, jargon, just spoken of an' known over there, locally, that is. – Is what our local fellahs who go there, tell us…" he tailed off, having nothing more to add.

Something else occurred to him. "We could walk along the beach and over the rocks to Perch Rock? You know, the fort!"

"Yeah," said one, scratching his bonce and starting show interest.

"Think a shullin', will cover it – the fare an' that?" piped up a lad sitting on the pub entrance step.

"Mm," he considered. "One-and-six or(7p) – better still: a florin.(2/-10p)"

A brief silence unfolded. "Better'n hangin' around this dump all day, doin' nothing'," said kerbside.

A bright voice suggested, "Bring our cossies-n'-towel?"

"Course!" he assured, pointing to confirm that late proposal was a good I-dea!

"But us's not goin' to the swimming' baths. Not this time."

The interest for the trip ratcheted up. They warmed to the idea, and it was not the sun in a cloud-less sky that added or supported the suggestion.

Before they started to split up, he told them. "Don't forget to make your sarnies, to take with us, yeah?"

There was a combined shout of agreement, saluting a sound brainwave.

The quartet were pleased to note, when they leaped off the step of the No.29 tram in front of the Liver Buildings at the Pier Head, before it had completely come to a halt – as usual, that there was a keen breeze blowing down river, and that the water looked quite choppy, even though it was fast flowing.

They leaned on the railings fronting the river below. Paused and peered down at the landing stage, where the tide showed evidence, with flotsam circling on its surface, that the tide was coming in.

"My dad reckons," said one of them staring down at the river's moving surface, "that the tide is about three knots and it comes-n'-goes in-n'-out, twice a day."

The others absorbed this information in silence.

"Which one of them ferries is the New Brighton boat?" Asked a voice at the rail and pointing down to the gaggle of ferries riding up against the stanchions of the landing stage, proper, awaiting captain's instructions.

"The Oxton and the Thurstaston are passenger ferry's, but the Upton is a luggage boat, with just the one deck. Lotta people down there, so they're probably using her because of her big crowd carrying space. Crowd more people on at one go. So," he breathed in quickly, "let's make a move, yeah?"

They didn't need any motivation or urging and headed almost at a run down the tunnelled gangway onto the swaying landing stage to pay for and collect their ferry tickets, latching onto the moving throng.

"What you doin'?" one of the boys asked him, as he stooped, then squatted down at the roped-off opening to a companionway that led down to the engine room from the passenger deck.

"Just looking."

"For what?"

"Am interested. I'd like to become a ship's engineer when I leave school."

"You said," the boy disputed with a laugh, "that you wanted to be an engine-driver, when we talked about it the other day?"

"Yeah, I know. Well, things change. Ship's engineers see more of the world. Going to sea, sounds a whole lot better than driving the train from Liverpool Central to Chester."

"They goes further than that!" his companion argued.

"Right," he grinned back up. "But sailing the seven seas is so much more exciting, with all those foreign parts an' places to visit."

"Okay," putting that aside, his mate said. "What can you see?"

"Here," he invited, "get down closer to me and look down there," he added, pointing down into an intensely reverberating and noisy enclosure. "That there, is a – I think – a triple-expansion steam engine."

"Where d'you get them words from?"

"Got uncle's in the merchant navy."

"So, what's that thingy-me-jig?"

Embarrassed, somewhat, he grinned back. "Don't know, but it sounds great. Just listening to them talk about such things."

"So, what else d'you know about it?"

"Got twin screws."

"What's them?"

"Propellers. C'mon, you know what propellers are!"

Sly grin back.

Straightening up, he said. "Let's go see over the stern. Race You!"

The loaded ferry shuddered slightly, which promoted "oohs!" from some on its crowded decks, as the engine room revs subsided and the Upton Ferry gently glided and nudged it's way sideways against the huge rubber tyres hanging from the landing stage at water-level and took the weight of the ship as she ground gently against the New Brighton stage, crews exchanging ropes with other deck hands to hook on and around the mooring bollards, preparatory to the landing gangway crashing down noisily into place in order that the passengers could disembark and leave the ferry, which they did in a 'torrent' and vigorously stepping out as a swamping tide of humanity, as soon as it was safe to do so.

"Hey, look at that fellah, high up on the road ramp from the landing stage. Look it – What's he gonna do?" one of his mates shouted, pointing up excitedly, but still aboard the ferry, staring keenly at a figure braced and stood perched on a metal spar, part of the construction of the bridge ramp.

"Hey, 'E's on'y got one leg, too!"

They stared across to the figure as he was poised on the outer edge of the framework, before he suddenly plunged off and down into the swirling waters of the river below, striking the water with a splash and immediately submerged.

Was there, one minute, and gone, the next.

"Was he puttin' on a show for us?" they discussed animatedly with each other.

"'Course he was. My mum's seen 'im before, an' she doesn't like it, 'cause she said it's dangerous."

"Is he allowed to do this?" another questioned.

Nobody knew the answer to that.

"Does he do this every time the ferry docks?" ventured another.

Nobody knew the answer to that, either!

They joined the tail end of the crowd off-loading, walked up the ramp and glanced down to watch the diver, swimming safely away to the beach.

They halted, stepping to one side, as the crowd pushed past at the top of the ramp, where it opened onto a road, across which was yet another pub.

Time to glance up toward the amusement park, beyond the slope and entrance gate, at the side of the building.

"There usta be a tower on the top of that building up there."

"What kinda tower?"

"Like Blackpool tower, on'y it was higher, so'as I wus told," said one of the boys. "My mum, said her dad – me granddad – went up it, once. That yous could see all the way to the Great Orme, Isle of Man and the Lake District from the top."

The four stared up and across the intervening space.

"Did it fall down – collapse, like?"

"They pulled it down sometime after World War One, I wus told. Said it was unsafe, 'specially on windy days."

They headed across the road and entered the fair ground which was packed, but there was plenty of activity taking place for them to see and remark about, even if they didn't possess the 'readies' to pay for a mechanical ride or two. Didn't matter, they still enjoyed being there. Mesmerised by the roller-coaster for some time, especially at the girls in some of the cars, who squealed blue-murder in their delight as the car plunged down into the drop. There were coconut shy's, target stalls with cross-bows, to pause at and watch as people applied their skills. Then a hoopla stall, which again looked deceptively easy to play and win on, but wasn't, they noticed. They came to an untidy stop at the 'Wall of Death' and read the words printed in large letters on the side of the wood structure and eyed the still murals of motor-cycles-n'-riders in protective gear closely, and which were painted on the exterior walls. They could hear motor-cycle engines being violently revved, within.

"What's that then?" said one, curious.

"Fellahs on motor-cycles racing each other, riding up and around inside the circular space, and the riders horizontal to the ground, as well."

"Horizontal? – How'd they stay up?"

"Motion…speed of the bikes. They start-up from a ramp at the bottom, inside, and they launch themselves up onto the walls."

"Anybody been killed?"

"See – the words painted up on the side, reads 'Wall of Death'."

They stopped and stared, open-mouthed.

Previous voice, piped up. "Anybody snuff it, in there?"

He didn't get an answer because nobody knew.

They moved on, looking and commenting, laughing and pointing.

Said one. "Hey, see that fella with the blond girl, over there?"

All four turned and followed his pointing arm, hand and finger, at a couple in their late teens, with their backs to them.

"I jus' watched him pay for her an' himself to go in the waxworks chamber of horrors, an' she took one look and headed straight to the exit," he finished in a gulped explosion of sniggering.

"So?"

"He'd already PAID, when she pulled away and dived out!"

"So?"

"She wet herself, when she saw where 'e wus takin' her, that's why?"

"An' he was all snarly, 'cause he'd paid and wouldn't get his money back."

With that explanation, all four continued to stare after the verbally arguing young couple, as they walked out of sight and were swallowed up in the crowd.

# 33. Liverpool's 'Coney Island' Part Two

After leaving the fair ground, they drifted along toward the open-air baths, which was not on their visiting list, this day.

"That a theatre?" one of them said, nodding his head across the road at a building set back from a stone wall, and a diagonal path with a line of benches looking out at the river scene, but all occupied with visitors, mostly old folks.

An old couple, passing, overheard the remark and stopped to confront the boys.

"Used to be a band playing at weekends in them gardens at the back," the cheerful husband with a shock of grey hair showing under his cap, hauling his wife to a halt, told them. "Then they covered it over in nineteen twenty-five and called it the Floral Hall."

The boys giggled good-naturedly at the intrusion as the couple smiled briefly and continued on their way.

The beach was in front and below them, onto which they headed down the stone steps. Having first found a secluded spot, which was hard to do, and covering each other with their towels from prying eyes, they quickly disrobed and pulled on their cossies, wrapping the shoes, socks, short pants and undies in their towels.

They made a bee-line for the lighthouse, across the sands and to the foot of the Anglesey granite structure, painted in white. They stepped around it, staring up at the sheer height of all its ninety feet or so, to the glass cover over the 'candle' that used to signal a warning to ships approaching the river mouth and it's narrows, at night.

"Eat our sarnies, now, yeah?" he suggested to the other boys, pulling out his brown paper bag wrapped package, but to the amusement of his cronies, because when he unwrapped them, they were a soggy wet mess, with no resemblance to what might have been called 'sandwiches'.

"Aw-wow, what 'ave you made them with?" a voice shouted into his ear, toothy smirks all around.

"Tomatoes," he managed, glumly, not one bit amused.

"Jeeze – you got a spoon with yuh?" cackled one, bending forward for a closer glimpse.

"Bloody awful," he agreed, mortified by the transformation.

"Won't go to waste," he was interrupted.

"Will, as far as I'm concerned!" starting to roll the paper bag into a lumpy wet ball.

"No, no," smirked an acute observer of nature.

"What?" he said, darkly, still holding the wet lumpy mass.

Smirker pointed to a waiting and watching group of yellow-eyed herring gulls not ten feet from where they stood. Their white heads with yellow beaks swung from left to right, vigilant as they had foreseen events unfolding and which told them that a much sought-after throw-away snack was in the offing, and which they – or rather, their powerful beaks – could make short work of.

He scowled down at the parcel in his hand, a baleful hasty glance, before unrolling the dark wet brown and now torn, paper bag. He pitched the contents into the air with one quick throw in the direction of what had now become a colony of hustling, fighting, frenzied, snatching and competing predators. The contents of the bag never landed on the sand and rock but were interrupted in mid-flight and subsequent descent – and vanished! vigorous thrashing and shrieking from the gulls as they fought for the last sloppy morsel.

One of the boys stuck out his arm towards the unfortunate sandwich-maker.

"Yous can have a suck of my ice lolly, if you wants?" the kind hearted bessy-mate offered, generously, but was not followed up.

Further along the sands, they halted at the foot of the Fort Perch Rock and contemplated its visual aspect of red sandstone construction. They had time to meditate and ponder its original purpose.

"When was this built?" echoed one, aloud.

"Dunno," seagull feeder managed, disgruntled still. "Middle of last century – something like that?"

"What for?" a sing-song voice, yawned.

"To protect 'The Pool' from a French invasion."

"Napoleon?"

"Yep, but that was before he got whipped by us, at Waterloo."

"So, why build it?" sing-song continued.

"Well, they'd got this idea before Waterloo, an' so they just went ahead, in case – I s'pose – it might be somebody else, who'd invade us."

"Who?"

He knew in his water, one of them would ask that question and shouldn't have elaborated. He rubbed his forehead to produce an answer and frowned, hard.

"I don't know – the Yellow Peril!" he grinned back, sheepishly.

"Who's that? C'mon…"

"Oh, the – er, Japs or the Chinese."

"What?" another of his mates, jumped at reply. "In their Junks?"

"I'm not a blooming history teacher, am I. How would I know?" he snapped back.

"Alright, alright…" Giggled the wit. "Keep yer 'air on, I on'y asked!"

They were on the move again, drifting along the shore line and gradually approached and passed under the decking and bridge of the New Brighton landing stage. Now, pausing and watching with some interest, as ferries arrived disgorged their transported masses and left again, equally crowded, destined for Liverpool's Pier Head.

The quartet stepped along and beyond the under section, toward the sandy, but now rocky shoreline that reached toward Wallasey town hall frontage. Stopped for a moment when abreast with the slope leading to the funfair and overlooked by it, with all the attendant sounds of lively organ music, excited screams and cries of people enjoying some of the amusement rides.

Suddenly, the boys noticed the almost hysterical concern of a distressed woman in her thirties, about thirty feet ahead of them, shouting out and gesticulating frantically to attract the attention of someone at the rippling edge and whirling eddies of the river. The moving waters were starting to make inroads as the tide changed and the current rushing and swirling in from the bay, forming small eddies and widening its width with each successive swamping flow.

The object of her frantic waving was a four-year-old on a now isolated sandbar, the rush of incoming tide cutting him off from his very anxious parent.

It took only a few moments for the quartet to size-up the increasing danger.

Lousy sarnies were forgotten about as he thrust his bulky towel into the hands of the nearest mate; then bounded into the rising gully of incoming tide and toward the stranded youngster. He quickly forded the knee-deep flow and emerged on the sandbar.

"Hey, gimme your hand," he shouted at the perplexed infant. When he didn't respond, he reached and grabbed at a wrist and tugged him around, yanking the child behind him to retreat back into the fast-moving current. He then suddenly realised the immediate threat, which was instantly confirmed when he found the moving water had risen way about his knees and was now at thigh level and pressing against him, making headway slower even as his toes dug into the loose and shifting sandy bottom. He quickly realised the water would be up to the child's chest, so turned and snatched the little fellah up from the deepening flood and onto his hips, as he whirled and continued through the ever-pressing torrent.

Seconds later, his feet were on dry sand and he dropped the youngster onto a clear space at his side. The child ran, dripping river-water, straight toward his anxious mother outstretched arms.

"Thanks, lads," she shouted and turned away, but head lowered to verbally chastise the youngster who protested his innocence, arguing back and giving her a loud of old buck!

"My mother would've given me a slap, for that," one of the boys soberly observed.

"Phew! That wus close!" towel holder said, returning it to him.

"Yeah, good job we wus nearby," concluded another of the gang, casually.

The incident was immediately dropped and forgotten, as pressing pangs of hunger raised its more demanding head.

### War News!

- US Marines and army units, backed up by a mighty armada of American warships, including many aircraft-carriers carrying supporting squadrons of dive-bombers and fighters, stormed ashore from landing craft at the Japanese island of Okinawa, as part of OPERATION ICEBERG. This, the largest and most complicated amphibious landing launched in the Far East during WWII. This invasion is the prelude to the final and ultimate invasion of the Japanese mainland.
- British Task Force 57, consisting of four large and six escort aircraft carriers, were charged with attacking Japanese airfield installations in the Sakishima Islands to prevent them from reinforcing Japanese attacks against the US landing areas on Okinawa,

ensuring they too, became targets of Japanese kamikaze air attacks.
- Sudden death is reported of United States President Franklin D. Roosevelt (32nd President of USA), who had recently visited and attended the Yalta Conference, with other leading Allied leaders, including Winston Churchill.
- British army liberates Belsen Concentration Death Camp in Lower Saxony, Northern Germany. They found approximately 60,000 Jewish prisoners living in squalid conditions and suffering variously from typhus, tuberculosis, dysentery and malnutrition.
- Russian army heavy artillery units begin long range shelling and pounding of Wehrmacht defensive positions on the outskirts of the German capital, Berlin.

## 34. A Dog on the Wall!

Nobody at home!

He stood looking out of the back kitchen window and stared at next door's black-n'-white terrier called Terry, up on the wall at the back of the house. That's right, he confirmed to himself, a dog traipsing along the top of the sandstone wall at the rear of their property on September Road.

Not a flat surface, but a bevelled top, no less.

How did the little mutt keep his footing?

It was, he told himself, amazing. Better still, remarkable. Liked the sound of it. An adverb, from the French, meaning 'worthy of notice'. He'd looked it up in the dictionary in connection with a composition he'd had to write, as part of last night's homework.

Thing was, about this dog-on-the-wall: it wasn't supposed to be there. He'd never seen, nor heard or been told, even, about a dog – any dog – that padded along a back garden wall, like this one did?

First time he'd caught sight of this curious circumstance and its antics through a back bedroom window, was when he was idly gawping, in a bored sort of way, preoccupied with his own thoughts, soon after the family had moved in. He was quite surprised by its spree, especially as the little mutt didn't know it was being spied upon, even if accidentally so. Had seen it leap – more like a spring-up, onto a low wall, further down along the backs of the houses, and fully expected it to fall off and tumble down. When it didn't, realised just how sure-footed it must really be. Like a wild goat on a mountainside? His eyes followed it as it continued its movements and ran along the low wall, which then sloped up almost abruptly, onto the higher back wall, which bordered and enclosed all the gardens behind the houses, which were in line. He continued to watch as it paused and sat down easily on its narrow bony haunches to jerk its head around inquisitively, small round eyes like two spiky black beads taking in the scenery and anything that moved. Jerky head movements, left-n'-right, up-n'-down! Watching the birds?

The local feline society didn't like it.

In fact, he's seen a head-on confrontation only the day before, when a ginger-Tom and the terrier met on the same piece of top wall, and there was a face-off at about ten feet!

The terrier, at first wagging his tail in a 'Hello, and how are you?' engaging disposition, but then immediately noticing that the Tom was not best pleased about his presence, barring the pussy's right-of-way.

Tom's long bushy tail was wagging too, but not in a palsy-walsy sort of way, but snaking from side-to-side, and starting to murmur in low menacing deep-chested rumble and from the back of his throat, hunched and coiled, prepared to spurt forward in a most unfriendly aggressive manner. Not anything like, and definitely not a nice-n'-friendly proper purring pussy!

The mutt's tail stopping wagging and became frozen in recognition of what was coming across the intervening space. Almost instantly – very quickly – the terrier's apparent friendliness evaporated and defiance took its place. His apparent slow-wittedness, didn't help. The unhappy feline immediately displayed immovable decisiveness. There was a display of evil intent and purpose, to stand his ground, forcing the terrier to decide against pushing his luck!

A stand off!

The puzzled mutt thought better of testing Tom's baffling refusal to give way, and like jumping off the wall to make way, which he wasn't about to – and didn't.

The little terrier lowered his head and sniffed at the empty wall between them. He sought to turn around in a very tight area, not without difficulty. This was due to the moss-covered small cryptogams clinging atop the sandstone bevel, not helping any in ensuring any kind of surefootedness and grip, as he began to twist about and commence a respectful withdrawal, with one back leg slipping off into space. There seemed no alternative in the face of this feline aggravation as he sought to extract himself from this difficult situation, but not without the trickiest of about-turns he'd ever attempted, But turn, he did, and successfully, finally showing his bum to Tom before he had managed to compose himself and prepared to move off.

He was immediately faced by a black moment…

Unforeseen, another frowning, threatening and evil-looking feline had suddenly materialised behind him and crept into position on the wall, cutting off his retreat.

Trapped!

He took the only possible line of action open to him: jumping nimbly off the wall to land in the soft soil of a back garden flowerbed, and scampered toward the side of the house, without looking back to and through the inviting open side gate which led toward September Road.

The great escape accomplished.

His dignity, intact!

He decided that the little mutt was one smart dog, and no doubt about it.

The two cats stalked each other head-to-head and rubbed noses, triumphantly.

He turned away from the window and let his eyes wander around the room. He was home alone and that was always good, 'cause when Mum was here, she'd keep him busy, like tapping on the living room window from the back garden, when his head was in the pages of his latest Hotspur comic.

"I want you to come outside," she'd form words with her mouth and lips, silently through the panes.

He'd smile back hiding the real him who thought it the most inconvenient time to call on his involvement at something he didn't really want to know about and dragging – forcing him to break off – during his favourite read. The 'charms' of gardening were all around him, Mum explained, as she sought to install her 'green fingers' attitude into the mind of No. 2 son. Weeding the flowerbeds was not a task that fitted comfortably into his chosen pastime.

Not, ever!

Mum would always insist, "You can read that comic, some other time – like, when it's raining, f'r instance…"

Pray for rain…

Dad seemed to be at work, most times, but when he was home, he'd snooze in the armchair to catch up on 'forty winks' from hours of lost sleep. Awake, he was pleasant and always willing to discuss any popular topic or controversial subject.

As a result, it helped him develop his own form of applied logic, especially with the other kids in the road. He found, he used his dad's comments to force home his argument and help him win over different views on the corner of the road, during impromptu chit-chat.

Leastways, right now, he had the house to himself.

He stepped up to the wireless, resting on one end of the sideboard. Was the accumulator battery still charged up? Relieved, it seemed to be a-okay which was fine, until it was time to change it at the end of the week. He reached up a hand and turned the switch to 'on'; then flashed the broadcasts dial.

…Richard Tauber singing 'You Are My Heart's Delight', not the singer or the song that attracted him. In fact, he couldn't understand what people – grown-ups – saw in him? However, he kept his thoughts to himself, because Mum was of the opinion that he was a marvellous vocalist. He'd heard her say so, and that was why he kept his trap shut. On the other hand, Bing Crosby crooning 'Swinging on a Star' was definitely a winner. Another moan-n'-groan Mum liked was Donald Peers painfully depressing young people's delicate hearing, to 'In a Shady Nook, by a Babbling Brook'. On the other hand, he kind of liked the Mills Brothers singing 'Paper Doll'. Was original, he decided. Moreover, there was Geraldo and his orchestra and their recording with Johnny Green singing, 'McNamara's Band'.

Great tune!

He couldn't understand why a soldiers' audience, he'd seen on a Gaumont British News film Clip at the Pictures, applauding Vera Lynn singing that soppy song 'White Cliffs of Dover' so enthusiastically?

# War News!

- Russian armies link-up encirclement of Berlin, as the Soviets strengthen their grip on the remaining German defenders.
- Benito Mussolini, his mistress and henchmen, are captured and executed by Italian partisans.
- Elements of the Anglo-Indian British forces in the Far East, capture Rangoon.
- Adolf Hitler and his wife, the former Eva Braun, commit suicide in the Berlin bunker, together.
- Soviet flag is flown over the Reichstag Building in Berlin, as the city surrenders to the Russian onslaught.
- Reich President, Carl Dönitz, former German Grand Admiral, surrenders unconditionally to Allied Forces in the West.
- Japanese air force planes press home further kamikase attacks against the American naval fleet supporting the landings on Okinawa.

## 35. Ve-Day, Followed by a Night of Flaming Torches!

"You must've heard?" one of his mates, hugely animated and in joyful mood, shouted to him from across the road.

"What?" he questioned, about to step up the side path to his house.

"War's over, mate!" the kid across the road, happily confirmed.

"Knew it was about to happen," he shouted back, "Monty meeting the German generals, an' all that," he further agreed.

"On the wireless," mate informed, crossing the road to join him on the pavement. "At midnight, last night."

"Great news, then!"

"Smashin'. An' not only that, there's gonna be a celebration with a bonfire down the bottom of our road, tonight."

"Tonight?" he repeated, to be sure of his facts.

"I'm goin' down the road, this afternoon, to help collect wood-n'-stuff, to burn on it."

"Right," he nodded.

"See yuh there…" said his mate as the boy began to break into a run down the pavement toward the bottom of the road, to where he lived.

"See you?" he shouted back as he turned and retraced his steps up his side path to the house, expecting Mum to have made him a lovely tea, or leastways, was in the process of making it – preparing it?

Mum was in the kitchen attending to pans on the stove, which were steaming as the contents boiled. The wireless was on, broadcasting a popular song.

"Did you know the war was over, Mum?" he laughed as he stepped in through the back kitchen door.

"Doesn't everybody?" she answered with a smile.

"Well...I do, now."

"Was on the wireless, this morning," she told him. "The Prime Minister – Winnie, said that the War in Europe was over, but we still had to prepare for the defeat of Japan."

"Oh yeah," he observed, caught out. "I'd forgotten about the Japs."

"Here," Mum said to him, passing clean plates from her hands to his. "Put these on the table and get out the knives-n'-forks from the drawer."

This day, Monday, May 8, 1945, was like no other on September Road, in Liverpool. Come to think of it, he guessed, this same application would apply to all other streets, roads and avenues in not only this wonderful city, but all and every other town as well, nation-wide! The more he thought about it, the more he realised he'd short-changed his conception, because this would be a HAPPY DAY for all people in all countries involved in backing and support of the Allied cause in Europe. Even, maybe, a day of prayed-for relief that it was finally over, for those unfortunate people who'd lived under the heel and jackboot and the Swastika!

"'Specially, those poor people rescued from the German concentration camps when the Allied troops reached them," he commented.

Or was he a tad too dramatic, listening to too many radio plays?

He almost ran down the road, after his tea, and soon picked up with his mates, some of whom were already gathering spare and discarded wood for the construction of the bonfire, which was due to be lit, come twilight, he was told.

"There's tons of old lino in that Entry," one of the boys gleefully shouted in his direction.

"For the bonfire, yeah?" he concluded.

"No – No, to make fire torches," his mate confirmed.

He dashed after his fellow September-Road-ite, to learn precisely what the lino was intended for?

"I told yuh," the boy halted, breathless, and in order to gather up loose scattered pieces of splintered timber lying around on the spare ground at the bottom of the road.

"How d'you do that?" he asked, mystified.

"Them fellahs in the Entry, over there, will show yous."

He glanced back toward the Entry and caught sight of older boys – teenagers – ripping the floor linoleum into long ragged four-to-six-inch-wide strips; then binding them tightly as they could around hatchet handle-length sticks or baulks of cricket bat long splintered timber, before hammering it home with nails to ensure the material remained in place on the end of the handle, once it was set alight.

Already, a pile of these 'torches' were beginning to build up on the ground and against the brick wall at the side of them.

One or two teenagers glanced up as he arrived close to them, questioningly.

"Me mate said to come over and' help?" he told them, grinning.

A teenager working there pointed at the torn length of ex-kitchen floor lino, awaiting attention.

"Yous can start cutting' that lot inta strips," the teenager said, pointing to an untidy pile of torn rolls, "same-as width, we're usin'," the older kid added.

He got straight to work with a gusto, pulling a dirty, torn and dusty roll off the top of the pile and dragging it to a free space, where he'd start to cut it into lengths.

Easier said than done, he realised once he'd started, as he first laid the roll out and flattened it on the Entry cobblestones, treading it out. It was a piece of frayed and very worn old linoleum.

To start with, the knife edge was blunt, or near as dammit. Needed a lot of elbow grease just to get it to bite and begin to part an irregular strip, about five inches wide.

He shouted to the teenager he'd spoken to. "This knife won't cut."

"So sharpen the bleedin' thing," was the retort.

"On what?" he threw back.

"If it's too hard for yous, leave it and go collect wood for the bonfire," the lad shouted to him, before recommencing to cut another strip into folded pieces, which he had then slotted over the head of a wood baton, holding it in place, underfoot. The lad then adopted a kneeling posture and placed a rusty nail about the middle of the shaped rolled lino; then hammering it through, with an old cast-iron hammer and into the head of the stick, throwing the finished product onto an already growing pile of 'soon-to-be' fire torches. This was all planned when the sun had gone down, darkness had descended, the bonfire lit and the torches put to the use for which they were made and intended.

Resting for a moment, leaning against an adjacent low wall, fronting the houses lower down September Road, he took in the change in people's habits this particular evening. Stood to one side at the bottom of the road, he watched as more and more grown-ups stepped out of their homes, meeting and cheerfully chatting with their neighbours on the pavement. This was something different, something more than normally seen or expected. And, of course, events were unprecedented, so it was perfectly understandable.

No worried, glum or depressed expressions.

No furrowed brows.

No more family worries about family in the Forces and their being wounded or killed in battle – in Europe, leastways.

There was, however, – and he'd overheard, eavesdropped on adult conversation, that there was concern about the struggles that lay ahead, especially regarding the invasion and battle casualties the American and our British services had estimated and were expecting, as a result of the final outcome in subduing fanatical Japanese resistance to any landings on the Japanese mainland. Everyone – kids included – were aware of the suicidal tactical reaction of the Japanese character in war.

However, no matter, people seized on the opportunity to enjoy themselves and the end of the war was a good enough reason, as any and the best.

He was jolted back to the present, by a heavy hand on his arm, as the familiar face of a mate appeared at his side.

"They're gonna light the bonfire. Are yuh comin'?" the youngster shouted nosily into his ear.

"Oh, now?"

"See…it's dark enough. We can fire up our torches, yeah?" the mate said, eyes dancing.

He nodded agreement, filled with sudden expectation, as he saw and heard the bonfire being lit. There was a burst of cheering and "Hoorays!" from the kids and "Hoorahs!" from much older people grouped and stood about on the pavements. Old newspapers bundled at the base of it were set alight by struck and thrown on matches, lighters and thrusting lit tapers, followed by further squeals and cheers of those closest as the flames took hold.

The different-coloured fingers of flame soon leapt skywards amid the dry concentration of paper and wood, licking up the sides and as a slight breeze blew, the base glistened red, and burning wood could be heard to crackle as the fire increased into roaring volume of wild sounds, the conflagration spreading and taking hold.

Singing broke out from several uncoordinated voices around the flames. Some, the first verses of the national anthem, *God Save Our Gracious King…* and others, *Land of Hope and Glory*. Sporadic cheers mixed with laughter, broke out from various groups stood by. A kind of temporary lunacy seemed to have taken hold, as local residents dragged out more old and battered items of furniture, to throw onto the edges of the bonfire and feed the flames.

He stood, almost transfixed, at the spectacle and scenes taking place, and for a moment was moved by the unnaturalness of what was happening at the foot of September Road.

"Light yer torch," a mate shouted next to him, brandishing an already lit flaming and burning poker.

He raised his stick with attached and loose flapping lino, and the moment the fiery torch touched his, there was a brief appearance and spit of grey/black smoke followed by a yellow/red flared flame, which licked over and around the business end of his home-made torch stick.

"There yuh go!" said the mate, who turned and raced away to join the others around the fire.

For a moment, he watched the flame take hold on his torch; then raising it above his shoulder, raced off to join the group of mates dancing in red-Indian style around the flaming bonfire.

What a fantastic time this was!

He felt, when joining the delight of others, that this was a sort of madness…

There was a cost!

He should've concentrated on what he was doing, because he'd always been warned, as a youngster, about how dangerous a naked flame can become.

He should've noticed the little flaming spots of burning black liquid shaking off his torch and spraying down onto the road surface.

He now paid the price for not being alert and focussed!

The back of his hand holding the torch aloft, suddenly felt the immediate pain of burning tar, as it slid and cascaded off the flaming lino and dripped down onto the exposed skin on the back of his hand, where it became a bluish/yellow inch long narrow low skin-level flat flame, where the base of his thumb joined his first finger.

He instantly released the torch, flicked away, down onto the roadway surface. He snatched back his hand, now feeling the full fury of the penetration of searing scorching hot tar burning a flesh wound, caused by the drip of burning tar drops onto the unprotected skin of his hand.

He headed home, darting headlong up the road, holding his right hand pressed tightly against his chest, the excruciating pain now almost unmerciful, as it penetrated, forcing tears into his eyes.

### War News!

- Allied forces capture Mandalay in Burma, from the Japanese.
- RAF mounts 1000-bomber raid on the German city of Essen, causing considerable damage.

## 36. Election Fever

Talk at the dinner table, that night, meandered onto the subject of the forthcoming planned UK General Election, which was something of very little interest and concern to his young mind and very much a grown-up's subject.

Mum finished eating, and got up to clear away the dirty dishes, so she could wash up and dry; then put them away in the kitchen cupboard. What she really wanted to do, was take her weight off her long-suffering feet after working all day, hemmed in, as they were, by wearing high heels. The luxury of putting her feet up, lighting a player's cigarette, starting to relax and then beginning to read the night's Liverpool Echo or Evening Express, was her ever-present desire.

He recognised that his mum had earned that right, and he welcomed and respected her need.

Curious and pursuing the search and desire for more knowledge on the election vote issue, had him say to his dad.

"You a Labour supporter? Really, Dad?"

"Of course!" he replied quite naturally, immediately, without any ifs-or-buts.

A straight forward answer to a straight forward question? His reaction to dad's instant retort, was a natural, "Why?"

Now, his father, paused. "Because, this lot are in power…"

"Still a coalition, isn't it?" Mum said without looking up from her paper.

"Not now, it isn't," Dad corrected. "It's dissolved. That's why we've got an election looming ahead of us, next month."

"Why Labour, Dad?" he persisted.

"Because, this lot, who are running the country, don't represent the working man."

"But isn't Mister Churchill the Prime Minister, anymore?"

"For the moment but won't be after the election."

"Thought you liked him?"

"Yes, the man for the job while the war was on, but not when we get the peace, and besides, it's the party he belongs to, that I don't trust for our future. They called the Great War, the war to end all wars."

"Who did?" he asked his dad.

"The government of the day. And when Tommy came home and was discharged from the army, there was no work – jobs for him to go to. Now, the war's virtually over or will be when we beat the Japs. The men will want a country fit for heroes, this time. What they'll want is a government in power that serves their best interests, not the capitalists who control where all the money goes – and it's not to the working class."

"Churchill wants the coalition to continue until we defeat the Japanese," Mum commented, taking off her apron and folding it.

"Clem…The Labour leader, didn't agree," said his dad, "and I agree with him."

"Clem?" the youngster asked.

"Clement Attlee. Leader of the Labour Party," he paused then continued, "When this war's over, the men coming back will want a greater share of the nation's wealth."

"Is that what happened after the First World War?"

"That's what I just told you a minute ago. They had the working classes go out and fight their war but gave us nothing in return after we'd won the war, shedding our blood for them. There was a lot of trouble after the Great War ended."

"What kind of trouble?" he asked his dad.

"Well, for starters, the police went on strike."

"Where?"

"Here…Here in Liverpool, in the August of nineteen-nineteen."

"Why was that?"

"Well, because of pay and conditions. Constables got less pay than farm labourers, at that time, worked long hours with almost no time off; weren't entitled to a pension until they'd got thirty years in, and not before. They got so unhappy, they decided to form their own union."

"So what happened?"

"I was in the army at the time, over in Germany, but I heard about it. Soon as some people – specially, villains, knew the Coppers were on strike, they broke into shops, pubs and warehouses."

"Shops?" his young eyebrows shot up.

Dad recalled. "Heard that some were even stealing just about anything. Eye-witnesses said they saw a mob in London Road, with snatched shop window models bobbing up-n'-down as they crowd went on the rampage…rolls of cloth on their shoulders and running away up side streets!"

"Really?" he managed open-mouthed and incredulous.

"Government sent the army in, and the Lord Mayor – or somebody in the town-hall, deputised civilian volunteers, with powers of arrest, to guard the remaining big shops and businesses, in town."

"That's one of the reasons I'm voting Conservative," Mum suddenly said vexed.

"Wasn't the Labour party's fault!" Dad objected.

"I remember those times." Mum frowned back.

So that was it. Dad supported a Labour vote and Mum remained loyal to her Tory blue roots.

Because it was a sore and sensitive – a contentious point between them, the conversation ceased and the topic changed to what Dad wanted for his dinner the following night?

Close to Election Day, he was asked by one of his mates, whose father was a Labour councillor or activist, to pass out political leaflets to grown-ups attending the local greyhound racing at the White City Stadium, one night, across Lower Breck Road, opposite the the Clarion pub at the top of September Road.

It was fine just handing out the printed labour election leaflets, helping out a mate whose dad had handed him a wad of these black-n-white pamphlets, at the foot of the wide concrete steps leading up to the main entrance. Made him feel important, until one middle-aged gentleman dressed in a suit with a collar and tie, stopped, accepted his handout and then went on to ask him if he knew what this election was all about?

He was caught on the hop and flat-footed.

He really didn't know but was tempted to tell him – reacting – that if his dad voted Labour, and it was okay for his dad; then it was okay for him, too!

He didn't, but shrugged his shoulders as the man turned away, smirking and shaking his head, before stepping up and continuing his steps to the entrance, to the Greyhound Stadium.

Slightly peeved at his own ignorance, he stared down at the Labour leaflet in his hand and tried to make some kind of intelligent sense out of the printed message to voters.

A BEVERAGE PLAN PRESENTED AS A COMPREHENSIVE MANIFESTO FOR SOCIAL REFORM

He grunted partial recognition that it had to do with most working classes, his dad talked about in the house, which included both his parents, but it…well nothing wrong with that, right? Sounded fine, he ruefully accepted, scratching his forehead thoughtfully.

THAT ALL WORKERS PAY A WEEKLY CONTRIBUTION, AND IN RETURN WOULD BENEFIT, ESPECIALLY IF THEY WERE OFF SICK, UNEMPLOYED, RETIRED OR WIDOWED.

He wondered about the weekly contribution and especially, how much?

But the rest of it, sounded fine!

NATIONALISATION OF INDUSTRY

Over his head? Thought the government owned the railways, coal mines and steel companies, anyway? They were producing and building the tanks, airplanes and warships, weren't they?

MASSIVE HOUSE BUILDING PROGRAMME WAS PROMISED, SO THAT EVERY FAMILY HAD A GOOD STANDARD OF ACCOMMODATION

Mm! He was aware and knew that during the air raids, a lot of houses were either destroyed by direct bombing hits, or severely damaged, with no windows, and all that.

A HEALTH SERVICE AVAILABLE TO ALL

Well, he mused, it was, anyway, yeah? He hadn't ever heard of anybody who was injured during the bombing, being turned away from the 'ozzey'?

Not sure he understood all of it in the leaflet. Leastways, he now had a hazy idea of what the Labour Party was promising, in order to get people to vote and support them into office. Sounded okay by him. And, if his dad was supporting them – they must be okay and honest-Joe's, because his dad wouldn't accept anything less!

In late July, the nation's newspapers printed the sensational news that the Labour Party had won the UK election in a landslide.

To him and his mates at the top of the road, playing footie, it sounded a complete bore!

**War News!**

- Russian forces invade Manchuria, driving Japanese army units before them into retreat.

## 37. Dad's Sidecar Peril

Dad and Mum visited the Jolly Miller public house on Queen's Drive to meet by arrangement in order to have a cheerful friendly drink and convivial chat together with Vee's parents. Although, Number Two son, was not present, he did get to hear about an 'incident' that occurred there, the next day.

Seems, from what he heard from Mum, that while they were at a table in the pub, Vee's dad – introduced to him as Uncle Jim – bumped into and met up with a friend of his. This stranger was clad in motorcycle garb, helmet, goggles, leather jacket, protective pants and lace-up jump boots.

Story goes, that motorcycle man had just purchased a second-hand motorcycle and sidecar. Was apparently very pleased with himself about the purchase, too. And whilst he was there and getting into conversation with Uncle Jim, Dad – out of courtesy – was introduced to him, as was Mum, at the table.

Stranger went on to let them know about his good fortune in just one afternoon, purchasing the combination at a rattling good price. How he'd brokered a good bargain and knocked down the seller's price to suit his pocket. Very proud about that, he let his listeners know. During the process of this friendly chin-wag, motorcycle man very kindly and generously offered to take 'his dad' on a short spin, as a nice little charitable gesture.

His dad, with Uncle Jim, accompanied the stranger to the car park, to view the recent purchase and were shown the highly polished and shiny machine.

His dad couldn't resist the kindly offer to go for a quick spin in the sidecar down Queen's Drive to Muirhead Avenue, and back, a distance of less that half-a-mile.

The women, meanwhile, resisted the temptation to view the motorcycle-n'-sidecar and instead had their men folk buy them a couple of extra gin-n'-tonics at the bar and brought back to the table, before they departed. They planned to continue their 'woman-to-woman' talk, while the men were outside, inspecting the purchase and engrossed in technical talk.

Seems that the men were into smiles all around, as Dad climbed into the cramped seat section of the sidecar to enjoy the short, exciting experience, before returning to the table, the 'girls' and getting back to the serious business of supping beer.

Motorcyclist climbed astride his mount, shut down the hood over dad, sat alongside, and then adjusted his goggles.

The engine of the combination ignited and roared into life.

Rider and passenger both gave Uncle Jim a brave jaunty smile and a curt wave come-salute.

The combination wheeled off the car park and nosed out into traffic on Queen's Drive dual carriageway; then roared smartly away, leaving a small cloud of exhaust tailpipe bluey-grey black, behind it in a hanging smelly smog.

Uncle Jim, the railway policeman, described later, that he watched them race off down Queen's Drive, make a U-turn at the distant traffic lights on Muirhead Avenue junction, then race back up the return carriageway, toward him.

"That," commented Mum matter-a-factly the following day, when back in her own home and sat at the table with her youngest son, "was when it all went wrong."

"Really!" said big ears at her side, excited to learn more.

"As the combination wheeled into the car park," she recounted, "from what uncle Jim, told me, it suddenly wobbled and the sidecar came adrift from the machine – broke away – from the motorbike and careered off into the hedge surround, with your dad in it!"

His eyes widened as Mum revealed the final result.

"And?" he gasped, eyes wide and urging more.

"Your dad fell into a crumpled heap inside the front of the sidecar."

"Oh, no!" was her son's outburst, hands up and covering both ears, in almost disbelief.

"Your dad had to be assisted – pulled out of the sidecar," she continued and shaking her head solemnly, lips compressed.

"Oh, wow!"

Mum was interrupted further, by the sound of a key being inserted in their front door.

Dad had arrived home from work, and his heavy footsteps could be heard pounding on the lino covering of the hall, headed in their direction.

"Can't sit here all day, talking to you. Must get the dinner on for your father," she said, both hands pressing down on the table as she rose to her feet.

Mum disappeared into the kitchen.

"Dad'll tell the rest of it, himself," she shouted with a half-smile, filling a pan of peeled spuds with fresh water from the tap, with just a trace of a giggle, to finish off.

He waited while Dad came into the dining room and said a cheery 'Hello' to both of them.

"Is the dinner on?" he said, unnecessarily; then immediately picking up the evening paper to scan the headlines.

"Dad?"

"Yes, son," he replied from the printed page.

"Did…did you nearly get killed?"

That got a reaction. He paused in reading the printed columns, to glance up and across the room in the direction of the kitchen.

"Killed?" he echoed loudly.

Mum shouted from the kitchen. "Told him about your little…ah, remarkable contretemps, yesterday."

"Oh, that," he beamed, suddenly embarrassed at the disclosure, his eyes flashing back to read the list of horse-racing winners, that afternoon, in the stop press.

### War News!

- General Curtis LeMay, Commander of USAAF XXI Bomber Command, continues daily bombing raids against Japanese targets and cities including Nagoya, Yokohama and Osaka, ordering the dropping of incendiaries and high explosive ordnance from B-29 Flying Fortress bomber formations, making their

attacks from recently captured airfields, closer to the Japanese homeland, in the Pacific.
- Forward units of massed Soviet armies, enter and capture the city of Prague, as German forces retreat, fighting their way out of the western approaches, against encircling partisan insurgents, even though the war in Europe was officially over.
- German military occupiers in the Channel Islands, surrender and relinquish control of Guernsey, Sark and Jersey, to Royal Navy destroyers.
- Allied plans, previously discussed, arranged and decided upon regarding the division of Germany, between Britain, United States, Soviet Union and France, after the surrender of all German military units, are now put into force.
- Japanese forces suffer huge losses in men and material in defence of Okinawa.

# 38. School Treat for Ve-Day!

All kinds of excitement was being generated with the passing of VE-Day, and for sure, without special emphasis, he decided, no assertion needed, nor required.

The end of the war or wars was in sight.

European conflict was already finished.

Over!

The local Picture House newsreels paused before showing the full extent of the latest concentration camps horrors exposed, after their inmates had been rescued, liberated, by the Allied advance into German territory.

Parents with accompanying children, were urged to consider – if they thought it necessary to protect their young minds from the hellish graphic moving pictures – to take them out of the auditorium during the showing? These latest Movietone News sequences were captured by Allied cameramen when they entered the death camps on the heels of the invading British and American units, and which revealed the effects of in-human persecution and subsequent wreckage inflicted on a fenced-in minority group by pathological killers in black SS police uniforms.

He and a pal from September Road, were unaccompanied and their curiosity for the macabre, at thirteen years, was not to be denied. They remained sat glued to their seats in the stalls as some responsible mums heeded the newsreel advice and removed their youngsters along the rows, up the isles and into the foyer, momentarily, until the shots were over, and they could safely return to their seats for the running of the main feature, which was scheduled to follow, immediately everyone was re-seated.

He, and his mate, cringed as they stared up at the big screen when it continued, revealing single lines of human scarecrows in skeletal form, draped in dirty torn sheets of stripped pyjama-like disgusting coverings, the rolled bundles of rotting corpses, giant ovens blocked with blackened carcases, followed by long shots of rows of black-painted huts, within which – the cameras tentatively edging forward – showed barely alive human forms who lay in tight hemmed-in wood caged receptacles of fetid, vermin-ridden filth and stinking offensiveness.

The stench could only be imaged, as British soldiers, handkerchiefs pressed and covering nostrils, was enough of a clue.

It was more than they expected, and the horror of what these painfully barely recognisable wasted faces, with wide staring eyes – some whimpering openly – within the angle and scope of whirring camera lens, was difficult – no, impossible for them to comprehend.

The youngsters were looking at the tattered remains of a people whose only crime had been an accident of birth!

He averted his eyes, finally, and found his friend had done the same. They exchanged shocked and frightened unpreparedness. Upon mortified reflection and with nausea developing in his breadbasket, he wished he'd given the newsreels a miss.

Something was up, he was sure of it, because the whole school, that particular morning had been ordered to assemble in the top classroom. They were gathered, as near as possible into the space vacated by chairs and desks, temporarily shunted aside to make way.

Headmaster 'A-hemed!' loudly, followed by an immediate barked cough which cleared his throat in preparation for his announcement. He was stood before them and at the head of the room and attracted their immediate attention, silenced the tittle-tattle of chit-chat. He briefly addressed them on the subject of the Allied victory against Hitler and his Henchmen, and the ending of hostilities on the Continent, and then proceeded to tell them that the 'Liverpool City Fathers' in collaboration with the Education Committee planners had proposed and authorised a celebration of sorts: they will fund a free visit to a local venue of entertainment – to wit: a local flea-pit to honour this joyful event. This applied to all schools within the local city council area.

The Head, smilingly, further informed his audience, that as the 'powers-that-be' had left it to the discretion of local school Heads to decide on the venue, he – after much deliberation and discussion with his teaching staff – had arranged with the management of the Empress Picture House, in nearby Tuebrook, for the whole school to attend a showing of the latest British film of HENRY V, staring and directed by none other than Laurence Olivier.

There was momentary silence.

Suddenly coached by attending teachers, stood to one side of the room at the meeting, the audience was incited and encouraged to applaud the Head's wonderful announcement, but older lads were not so sure?

After school and returning home to September Road, in company with some of his classmates, they discussed the announcement. During the course of which, they met up with other mates who attended different schools and learned they'd been informed of this Education Committee masterstroke. Only difference was, their school had consulted and met with the full body of school children attending their meeting and had democratically voted to visit the Carlton Picture House at the foot of Green Lane, which would be screening a collection of 'Three Stooges' with ageless eye-poking and face-slapping routines, 'Abbott & Costello' with their rapid-fire repartee, sharply witty retorts, and Disney cartoon shorts, instead.

"Jeeze!" exclaimed one of his classmates, turning to him on the kerb of the pavement, in dismay. "Did yoos hear that?"

There were reluctant nods.

"Democratically voted on – did yis hear that, too?"

One or two shook their heads, dismally.

"Dixie was thinking this would be better," he commiserated. "Shakespeare is more…" he searched for the right word.

"Intelligent?" a voice interrupted, supplied with a scowl.

"Scholastic," he smirked back, sarcastically.

"Meaning educational, don't yuh? – You conk!" scored his mate in a sour return.

Come the day and the afternoon of the screening, the school had all trooped down to the Empress Picture House, carefully escorted by the teaching staff.

No matter the short-comings he'd expected, sat alongside his school friends, the film nevertheless turned out to be a lot better than a long yawn, as he'd anticipated.

Besides Larry Olivier as HENRY V, there were other well-known faces that the kid's recognised, such as Robert Newton playing 'Pistol', Leo Genn as the 'Constable of France' and Valentine Dyall as the 'Duke of Burgundy, but the latter better known as 'The-Man-in-Black' from the BBC radio-horror series, on the wireless.

At the end of the show, he and his friends – upon reflection – were moved by the battle scenes and found it all very exciting and stirring stuff, after all!

**War News!**

- HITLER DEAD!

# 39. Ve-Day and All That!

He had, with his mates, discussed the coming death throes of Imperialist Japan in the Far East, as they sat on, stood against or languished on the low wall fronting of one of the boy's houses on September Road, their usual haunt or meeting place where they could spout their own interpretation of news events without being overheard and corrected by grown-ups, during the early part of a day during the school hols.

They'd read the papers, listened to news broadcasts and heard their parents discuss where the war was up to.

They'd heard and followed the latest stories about servicemen abroad, returning early to the UK, after beating the Jerries on mainland Europe: being told, – and they, expecting this as their reward – only to learn to their dismay that their troopship had been redirected and was now destined for the Far East to join in some 'unfinished business'!

"Me dad said, our troops will 'ave to go in and land in Japan, and will end up fightin' the whole bloody population: woman-n'-kids, nans-n'-granddads, as well as all their soldiers…"

"And! And!" interrupted another, "Their airforce-n'-navy, don't forget!"

"No," the first kid disagreed, shaking his head knowledgeably. "Don't have no air force – all der planes wus shot down at Okinawa, and their navy is in Davey Jones's locker, after we sunk dem all."

"Yeah, well," the first kid bickered, "All them as is left. We'll haf ta kill the lot of 'em!"

"They won't kill the lot of them," he objected.

"Well, if our lads don't, they'll end up dead. – our lads, that is!"

Grim faces exchanged glances.

"They're bloody MAD!"

"We know that, carrot-head, but it doesn't change anythink."

"Bonkers!" laughed another, taken and amused by the use of the word.

"No laughin' matter, really," he cautioned his pals. "These Japs are not bothered about getting killed, like our soldiers would."

"You sayin', our fellahs are afraid?" objected one mate.

"My dad," he explained, "said they'd like to think they could avoid it in some way."

"Avoid what – getting' killed?"

Another voice blurted. "Wadda yuh sayin'?"

"That our solders don't go into battle to definitely get themselves killed; that they want to shoot 'em, injure the enemy and even maim them – kill, if they have to, but to try and come out of the battle in one piece and alive, so'as they can recover to fight again some other time."

Silence reigned while they pondered the reasoning behind all the arguments, which wasn't easy for them. One or two, frowned and pondered – acquiesced the result.

"Nobody wants to die, yeah?" he resumed.

There was a nodding of heads as they agreed with his words.

"The American president has sent a message from the meeting of all the Allied governments, after they met, to tell the Japs they gotta accept unconditional surrender. Like, giving them a chance to raise their hands and stop fighting a war they're not gonna win, in exchange for their lives."

"Makes sense," agreed one.

"And?" asked another.

"The message said that if they didn't surrender – give up – then the Allies will punish them!"

"Punish them?" a voice piped up.

"Annihilate them."

Another silence and a knitting of brows, broken by 'objector'. "Wipe dem out?

"'Course, dick'ead!" roared another vexed voice from the group. "What did yous think he bloody meant, arsehole?"

"Okay," protested 'dick-head', "what did they say?"

"Said they're not gonna."

'Old sage's' shook their young heads in disgust.

"So, whatever they gets, it's their own fault. Brought it on themselves by sayin' no."

"There's somethin' else," he said, to add to his last information from the Japanese government.

"What?"

"The American's have let it be known that they have got a secret weapon."

All eyes sped to him.

Chorused two or three, hoarsely. "Secret weapon?"

"A new bomb," he told the hushed inquisitive faces surrounding him.

"Bomb? What kinda bomb?" snapped 'objector'.

He shrugged his shoulders in response to the last question.

### War News!

- In a subsequent communiqué, it was learned that the Allied High Command were in the early stages of planning an invasion of the southern island of Kushu, or what constitutes the lower fringe of the Japanese Home Isles, in the spring of next year.
- American government shows its determination, in line with agreement with its Allies, to push and secure the unconditional surrender of Japan, to end and conclude hostilities at the earliest, in order to save lives both military and civilian. US government has therefore informed Gen Curtis LeMay, USAAF Far East Commander, of its decision.
- Washington has reportedly disclosed that a B-29 Flying Fortress dropped a nuclear device on the Japanese city of Hiroshima on August 6, as a result of the Japanese government's rejection of an earlier unconditional surrender demand by the Allied Powers.
- It later revealed that a United States B-29 dropped a second nuclear device on the Japanese mainland city of Nagasaki on August 9.

Kids in the neighbourhood were all excited by the news and met to discuss this new development or phenomena in aerial warfare.

"Told you the Americans had a secret weapon," he reminded his mates, who readily nodded.

"Tens of thousands were burned alive, someone said," one of the boys volunteered.

"With just one bomb?" questioned another.

"S'right! Was in one the newspapers. I read it myself."

"What kinda bomb, was it?" interrupted one of the mates scratching his head and frowning to understand.

"An atomic bomb," he confirmed. "Just one bomb, from one plane, on one city."

"God, what a shocker!"

They all agreed.

"What's gonna happen next?"

"That's what the Allied governments will be askin' themselves. Like, will the Japs surrender, now this 'as 'appened?"

Objector, from a few days ago, said, "Won't make no difference. Them lot will still fight on to the death."

"D'you think so?"

"Know so," he confided, tapping his temple with his index finger to signal confirmation.

"I thought," posed another lad, "that them Jap cities had all been burned down, anyway, with them Yankee bombers dropping incendiaries?"

"These must've been the cities they missed, yeah?"

"So, if the Japs still don't wanna surrender, what will the Yankee air force do then?"

"Find another city, s'pose," argued objector.

"Looks like the Japs will be forced to give up?" one of his BB pals commented as they joined band practise under Holy Trinity church, that week night.

"Not so sure," he responded, examining his drum sticks. "Very stubborn people."

"Don't you mean their governors, are?"

"Whoever?"

"Toke, will be the next target, won't it?"

He frowned before answering. "The Allies will give 'em more time to think it over, is my guess."

"Then what?"

"Depends on their response to the ultimatum?"

"But, if they don't?" the other lad persisted.

"Won't get to that. If they don't respond, it'll be complete annihilation," he concluded.

"Maybe that's what they want, after those airplane suicide attacks against our fleet and all them Banzai charges?"

"We'll see." He shrugged.

"If they don't give in – the Japs, that is – it means we gotta invade Japan, and my dad – whose in the army – said there'll be more British and American lives lost, than has been in the whole of the war in Europe!

"Yeah, I've heard that myself." He agreed.

"My dad," the other boy continued, "said he'd heard there'd be a million Allied dead!"

"Gawd! That's terrible."

"How's it gonna get stopped?"

"The new bomb'll probably save a lot of our fellahs and Yanks from having to go in.

His mate nodded and added. "Damn right!"

# War News!

- It was reported on August 15, by an official Japanese government agency, that Emperor Hirohito has accepted the Potsdam Surrender Declaration, which was the outcome of the meeting previously scheduled in a Berlin suburb in late July and early August, attended by President Harry S. Truman, Britain's Winston Churchill and Clement Attlee and Soviet Leader Joe Stalin. That demand had been to call for the immediate unconditional surrender of Japan.
- Sept 21, 1945 – Senior officials and representatives of the Japanese military and civilian populace signed the unconditional surrender document aboard the American battleship USS Missouri moored in Tokyo Bay. Allied Far East Commander General Douglas Macarthur accepted and co-signed this historic document, concluding the official cessation of all military hostilities between Japan and the Allied Alliance.

## 40. Dad Got Sick

He could hear his dad upstairs in his parent's bedroom, a bitter, chest-shaking stamina-sapping spasm of coughing, yet again, even though earlier, he'd sat reading the latest copy of the Evening Express in front of a roaring fire in the downstairs living room, after his tea in early evening. He paused and looked up from his comic, at the ceiling above his head and listened, not a little concerned.

His healthy dad who hardly ever seemed to ail from anything.

The winter season was getting into full and nasty swing, with cold winds and persistent sheeting rain, battering the outside windows of the house.

He recalled at the start of his dad's illness, when he was downstairs in the living-room: he'd suddenly and unexpectedly have a bout of disagreeable coughing which would explode inside his chest and force loose phlegm up and into the passageways of his throat, causing him to throw aside his newspaper and to lean forward quickly to spit into the open fire, in the grate before him, and rid himself of this agitated eruption. It landed on the burning red coals, sizzled and hissed briefly for a moment, before it was gone. This was before he was compelled to take to his bed.

It was a painful and unpleasant cough because it not only affected his dad but made those around him uncomfortable and sorry for his plight at one and the same time.

He heard Mum advise him that she thought he smoked too much and that it wouldn't be a bad thing, if he cut down? This kind of comment sometimes caused an amount of tetchiness between them, that sometimes rumbled into argument, which increased his concern as they exchanged fierce words and because he didn't like to hear his parent's wrangling discord. So much so, that he'd sometimes leave the room and go upstairs, so he couldn't hear anymore. It was not nice to hear your own parents bickering.

More than that, it disturbed him to hear them quarrelling like that and especially over his dad's illness. Maybe, his dad could and should smoke less, but it didn't seem right or proper for him to say so to his dad. His dad might not take kindly to that kind of remark coming from him, besides, he was saddened by his dad's plight and wouldn't – couldn't say something that might hurt him, because he was already hurting. This was something that only his mum should chide his dad about.

He loved both his mum and dad. His mum in a different way to his dad, too. His dad, whom he privately regarded as a hero, being decorated with the MM in WWI, and also being a regimental boxer for his unit; although his dad did allow, once, that the reason he fought for the regiment in competition was because it got him out of fatigue duties, he might otherwise and normally, have to endure.

Nevertheless!

Dad was not one to ever complain about personal problems. Leastways, he'd never actually ever heard him moan about his physical health rundown, like picking up a cold or a cough, which he usually just shook off. He just got on with his life. So, as for the cough, he didn't allow that it was anything more than a case of too many ciggies.

This last week, however, his ill health seemed to be getting on top of him and affecting his general day-to-day living. When he coughed, there would be more than just some mucus needing to be cleared from the back of his throat, or sounded that way? On top of which, he'd be forced to take time off from work – which he'd be loathe to do – in order to nurse himself back to good health and regain his strength. He always seemed to be in work and never avoided going out early on the job, each and every morning, including working overtime almost every weekend.

The first real note of concern was when his mum said that Dad hadn't gone into work that day; that he had 'caught a chill' as she called it, and he needed to rest up in bed for a day or so. He could hear his dad's irritable and persistent cough sounding from his parent's bedroom and through-out the house. Sounded nasty to his young ears. He felt maybe he should go tell him so, express his concern, but Mum had forbade him, and insisted Dad get some quiet and to let him alone to sleep it off. He didn't push it, because he sensed his dad would get all embarrassed if he went into the bedroom to tell him how sorry he felt and the worry he had about his dad's cough.

He shuffled into his bedroom, the shut the door behind him, before changing into his PJs, but still couldn't shake his dreaded mental fear.

His dad, he knew, was poorly sick.

That much, evident by his father's shortness of breath, continuous stamina-sapping cough, followed by frequent spitting to rid himself of sickly throat-clogging phlegm. Even with the door shut, he could still hear his dad's racking cough, which was painfully shaking his whole chest frame, breath inhaled and exhaled in a rapid rasping wheeze.
He pulled the clothes up over his head and rolled onto its side and began an urgent prayer into his pillow:

*'Our Father, who art in heaven, hallowed be thy name…'*

That night, his sleep was disturbed once or twice, when he heard his mum going downstairs to make a cup of tea for Dad, or refilling the hot water bottle, which she'd thrust under the sheets and onto his side of the bed.

Next day, he must've been worse, because Mum sent for the doctor, who arrived late morning, after surgery. He wasn't privy to what passed between Mum and the family doctor, except that a prescription was written out for a new medicinal compound to treat a bad case of influenza.

He was sent to the Chemist shop immediately and returned post haste at a run.

Mum made Dad a hot drink and took the tablets upstairs to begin giving Dad the dosage.

It must've been serious, he guessed, because big brother was sent for, and was released on army compassionate leave, returning briefly from northern Italy.

Later, downstairs, he overheard Mum explaining to a close friend, who called at their home, that the doctor told her dad was gravely ill with pneumonia and needed constant care and nursing; that the hospitals were very busy, but in any case, his dad shouldn't be moved. He also heard his mum tell the neighbour that the medication was called M & B, a new chemical compound discovery which was very successful in dealing with Dad's complaint.

Although not much at praying, as was the way with most kids, he murmured a silent prayer at night under the sheets of his single bed in his darkened room and hoped for its success?

Was God listening?

The prescribed medical mixture was said to be of particular benefit to those suffering from pneumonia.

Its success was borne out by the fact that after the first full night and day of the dosage, during which his temperature soared frighteningly and he began sweating heavily, he reached and passed through the high point and then was on the mend.

Mum, in constant attention, although now she was getting the opportunity of a full night's sleep, for the first time after many sleepless nights.

After several more days, the affliction miraculously seemed to have left Dad, and with his mum's dedicated bedside efforts for him, which included: a bed bath, regular hot drinks, devoting herself to ensuring he lay comfortably and in a sleeping position, her added expertise in producing small, but regular, culinary delights and in a constant supply, in the believe that folklore myth 'feed a cold and starve a fever' was best. He started to recover, slowly and gradually. Mum purchased reading material like daily newspapers and even had the wireless taken upstairs and placed on his bedside table, which ensured his amazing and wonderful recovery.

Within a week, he said he was ready and able to return to work on the docks, although not completely recovered.

The house, seemingly brooding with a heavy shadow of family concern, roused after Dad got up from his sick bed and began to shrug off and shake loose from under its dampening and depressing shroud. Dad started to look different. Colour returned to his pallid cheeks. The curtains were pulled back to let in the pale, but welcoming, sun. Week or so later, he told Mum he was going into work, even though she disagreed with his decision: 'Too early,' her advice ignored.

Mum returned to work, too, after her attentive full-time preoccupation with his successful convalescence.

The house took on a more assertive air, became normal once more.

Silent, calm and settled.

His little prayer must've been heard?

Thank you, God!